The Honourable Catherine

The Honourable Catherine

A Sequel to Jane Sinclair

David Edwards

Copyright © 2021 by David Edwards.

All rights reserved. No part of this book may be reproduced in any form or by any electronic or mechanical means, including information storage and retrieval systems, without permission in writing from the publisher, except by reviewers, who may quote brief passages in a review.

ISBN: 978-1-956515-56-5 (Paperback Edition)
ISBN: 978-1-956515-57-2 (Hardcover Edition)
ISBN:978-1-956515-55-8 (E-book Edition)

Library of Congress Control Number: 2021918499

Some characters and events in this book are fictitious. Any similarity to the real persons, living or dead, is coincidental and not intended by the author.

Book Ordering Information

Phone Number: 315 288-7939 ext. 1000 or 347-901-4920
Email: info@globalsummithouse.com
Global Summit House
www.globalsummithouse.com

Printed in the United States of America

Other books by David Edwards:

If I should die
No greater freedom
Lethal legacy
The Fifinella log
The story teller
Jane Sinclair
Vengeance is mine
Tom – the adventures of a Portsmouth lad

Technical:

DIY Guide to international accreditation for companies Pt 1 & pt 2

•Reader's Choice Award

My thanks to Wikipedia for much of the research material, and to John Simkin for extracts from his article, Women and University Education.

CHAPTER ONE

"How about, 'Jane'?"

"Certainly not! That name will forever be sacred and unique to me."

Jane smiled as a blush suffused her cheeks "I suppose we could name her after your mother, Charlotte?"

"Then we would have to give her your mother's name – and as much as I love your mother I really do not fancy, Matilda."

Sir Charles and Lady Jane Cholmondelay (Pronounced Chumley) sat in beautifully ornate chairs in Jane's sewing room that overlooked the long driveway that led up to Fordingbridge Hall. Jane had taken over the estate finances not long after they were married. Charles recognising her business acumen had relinquished the job willingly. He concentrated on rotating the crops and finding more profitable ways of marketing the produce that was grown on their large estate; much of which knowledge he had learned from Jane's father who had been very progressive- although many of his ideas, such as planting by the moon phases, had met with strong resistance.

"Well, we will have to give the poor mite a name soon; she is nearly a month old now."

"All the servants call her, Poppet. That name is often used for an enchantingly beautiful child"

"It is also used to describe a small figure of a human being used in sorcery and witchcraft," laughed Jane.

"Oh! Well, that's out then."

"Oh dear, Charles, the entire household has been at it for weeks – and I am sure that Benson is running a book on it."

"Of that you may be sure." Charles laughed.

There was a slight pause whilst each sat with furrowed brow thinking. Finally Charles looked up. "Kate has a pleasant ring to it; and it cannot be shortened as so many names are."

"Yes. I also like Kate but it doesn't sound so good with The Honourable in front of it. How about The Honourable Catherine Cholmondeley? that has a pleasant ring to it." Which had they recognised it was without doubt an oxymoron.

"Surely we would have to pad that out a little?" muttered Charles.

Jane clapped her hands."That's it then. The Honourable Catherine Elizabeth Cholmondelay."

Charles, thoroughly spent, agreed. He gazed at his wife of three years with eyes that still shone with barely suppressed adoration; as they had done since he first saw her; rinsing her hands of blackberry juice in a small pond in the New Forest in Hampshire so many years ago. He recalled that she had removed her stockings, thinking that she was alone in her favourite spot; he smiled as he recalled her haste to replace her stockings and the blush that had suffused her cheeks. He was still amazed as he recalled her early struggles and of her successful rise to own two of the best garment factories in London. He let his eyes roam over her slender figure and could see no change from the woman he had loved all those years ago. Childbirth had not coarsened her body and exercise had restored her slim waist.

Her eyes reflected his love as she recalled having nearly lost him to slavers off Algiers and her subsequent near death when she heard of his apparent loss. He was still the tall, broad shouldered man with his barely suppressed shock of fair hair and dancing blue eyes – they made a dazzling pair. Their charm and wit endeared them to all.

Jane reached behind her and tugged at the silken sash that rang a bell in the nursery where the nurse, Agnes, was tending their son, Christopher; who had been born some fourteen months previously.

Agnes was the wife of the farm manager; she was a typical country woman of the time, well rounded with a happy smiling face and large breasts that had served her eight children well; the youngest being fifteen and quite capable of looking after himself she had jumped at the chance to augment the family income as a nurse to Jane's two children. Always happy and smiling she had a multitude of interesting games and occupations with which to absorb the two children; she arrived red faced with Christopher, who was shrieking with laughter, over her shoulder. Placing the child down on the carpet she curtseyed to Jane.

"Sorry, Milady," she stammered, "he always laughs when I runs with 'im. E'll quiet down in a minit."

Jane gave her a broad smile. "Please do not concern yourself Agnes, I like to see him happy. I have asked you here because Lord Chumley and myself have finally given our daughter a name."

"Oh, Lawdy! Everyone calls her, Poppet, it'll take some getting used to. Pray what is it, Madam?"

"We have decided to call her Catherine Elizabeth, which will no doubt be abbreviated to Kate in due course," she smiled, looking at her husband.

"Oh! That's lovely, my lady; but Benson won't be making a lot out of that – it was favourite with the staff," she laughed.

Jane smiled at her. "I should have known that the servants would have chosen a name – and that Benson would have taken bets on it."
Christopher who adored his baby sister, toddled over to her cot and reaching in tickled her under the chin, she gurgled with pleasure. If he could have done so he would have stated; but to me you will always be, Poppet. He tucked the blanket around her as he looked in wonder at his baby sister.

Jane smiled at the idyllic sight, "Now let us go and tell their grandmothers."

CHAPTER TWO

The months passed, as they tend to do and Christopher grew into a striking clone of his father. He was tall for his age and with his shock of fair hair and startling blue eyes he soon had all the servants doting on him. The only one seemingly capable of twisting him around her little finger was his sister, Katie, whom he persistently addressed as, Poppet, as soon as he was able to pronounce it - in spite of his mother's entreaties. If anyone could eclipse Christopher's star it was her. They were a dazzling pair, he resembling a smaller version of his father and she pressed from the same mould as their mother.

Playing in the nursery, Katie tended to be the prime mover in the multitude of games initiated by their nurse; her robust pursuit of victory in all matters often led to somewhat rough play on her part; occasionally terminating in her brother receiving a thump on the head with a wooden sword, or similar; on one occasion cutting his head causing it to bleed. The nurse intervened and began to scold her for being too rough. But her brother would not hear of it, he held a kerchief to the cut to stop the blood flowing as he defended her.

"It is alright, Aggie, she did not mean it, really. She is only a baby and doesn't know any better." His intent was to save her being scolded.

At this announcement, Katie stamped her foot hard on the ground and wailed, "I am not a baby am I Aggy?"

Chris walked quickly to her side and wrapping his arms around her. "Hush, Poppet, don't cry, I hate it when you cry."

She choked back her sobs and gave him a radiant smile and as far as her brother was concerned all was right with their world.

It was just after his sixth birthday when he approached his father's study and knocked firmly on the door; there was a slight pause and then his father called "Do come in."

Christopher walked to where his father was sitting behind his desk.

"Good morning, father, may I speak with you about something that has bothered me for some time?"

His father smiled, "Of course, Christopher," wondering what could possibly be bothering his son, and relishing his formality, so unusual for his age.

"It is regarding, Aggy, our nurse," he hastily added, "and a very good one she is. However, I feel that the time has come to cast away childish things." Here his father made a slight cough as he attempted to suppress a laugh.

"I would like a tutor. I would have raised the subject some time ago but I was concerned that Aggy may lose her job, and I would not like that."

Here his father broke in.

"Christopher! Agnes is well aware that at some period you both will grow out of a nurse and that her position would become redundant. She is well aware that the job is not a sinecure."

Christopher looked askance. "I am sorry, Sir, but I am not conversant with that word, would you please explain?"

"Certainly, Christopher! Sinecure is merely another way of saying that it is a job for life – and not a very onerous one at that."

"I see, Sir. Thank you."

"I can assure you, my son, that should, and when, I terminate Agnes' employment she will be well compensated. What do you have in mind?"

Christopher contemplated him for a while before replying, with a most earnest mien. "I think, father, that it is time for me to have a tutor if I am going to follow in your footsteps and get into Oxford."

"I see! Is that your intention? I have already listed you with Eton- and as a second choice, Harrow. There is a very long waiting list; both of which could prove to be an Open Sesame to the civil service and a whole range of top positions," he smiled.

"If you have no objection, father, I would prefer to make my own way by my own efforts."

His father looked hard at his son. "I am very impressed, Christopher," he commented huskily. Then with a smile, "if you are sure, it will save me a lot of money; those places are not cheap. I'll start looking for a suitable tutor, however your sister is only five years old, do you really think that she is ready?"

"Poppet is still happy to play games and waste her time, but as soon as she knows that I am having a tutor her competitive nature will force her to join me," he laughed. "She is so clever, father, I will have to really put a lot of effort into my studies to keep ahead of her."

He looked out of the window where he could see his sister skipping across the field towards the river where he knew she intended to try her hand at fishing. They had a private spot where in the security of a screen of trees she would remove her stockings and paddle; wriggling her toes in the rich mud of the river bed.

His father twisted in his chair to see what his son was smiling at. It was clear to all that a very special bond existed between his children; they seemed to sense what the other was thinking, often saying the same thing simultaneously.

Chris turned back to discuss his education further explaining his reasons for not wanting to take the advantages of going to Eton, Harrow or even Charterhouse, which he had read about.

His sister had collected a small rod from the shed near the water and prepared the tackle. Had she known it that was the same rod that her mother had used when she challenged her father to a fishing contest many years previously. She laid the rod on the bank and sitting in the shade of a large willow removed her stockings, ensuring that she was not being watched as she slipped into the water, which was running fast after the recent rains.

Charles watched his son and listened to his summary with interest and pride.

Suddenly, in mid sentence, his son paused and his head tipped to one side in a listening attitude; then, without comment he dashed from the room and shot out of the front door like a scolded cat. He watched as his son scrambled over the fence enclosing the field and dashed after his sister.

Charles well knew of the telepathic bond between his children and realised that there was a problem and running to the stable where a groom was preparing a mount for him, he leaped into the saddle and galloped after his son.

Christopher barged through the tree line and seeing his sister struggling in the water leaped in without hesitation. Her head kept plunging under water as the strong current caught her; her dress had snagged on a large broken branch and she struggled to free herself; Chris dived under her and tore the dress loose, and holding her head up out of the water he struggled to reach the bank some ten feet away. His father, Charles, taking in the scene, leaped from his horse and waded into the water where he grabbed both his children and dragged them ashore.

Christopher checked his sister over carefully to ensure that she was alright and then for the first time he shook her and screamed in her face.

"Don't you ever do that again, do you hear me?" He shouted, his voice shaking with passion.

His father sought to intervene.

Just then Poppet drew in a deep breath and her eyes opened wide in disbelief as she burst out crying. Her brother was appalled as he gathered her into his arms.

"I'm so sorry, Poppet. You scared me, I thought I had lost you; now go and get changed or you will catch cold." He hugged her tight and kissed her tears away. She gave a dazzling smile of forgiveness and as usual all was right with his world.

His father lifted her in front of him to take her home; he paused a while for his son to join them, then understanding that his son did not want him to see his tears, even though they were tears of relief, he turned his horse and headed home. The story, oft repeated by the servants, lost nothing in the telling.

CHAPTER THREE

Over the following ten days interviews were conducted from 9am to 2pm three days a week. Most of the prospective tutors were sent from friends who no longer had need of them. The children were allowed to attend because as Christopher remarked;

"It is essential, father that we like them and realise their capabilities, or you could be wasting your money."

His father who had never found the necessity to talk down to his son was delighted at the maturity so apparent; and so it was that prospective tutors were somewhat surprised on being shown into the room to find themselves confronted by the entire family. Some found it daunting; others were delighted to get a glimpse of their charges before committing themselves. Charles, who was well aware of his wife's business acumen often deferred to her. The children were more concerned with appearances; whether they looked pleasant and friendly. Chris' comments once the tutor had departed was on those subjects that interested him whereas his sister tended towards an instant liking or disliking

The applicants were an eclectic lot, predominantly male who flaunted their qualifications with pride – one was an elderly chaplain who was obviously looking for a sinecure in which to finish off his remaining years in comfort; another was a very pompous middle aged man who was prone to air his opinions rather than answer the questions put to him. Jane was particularly taken with a young woman just twenty five years old who informed her that she had just qualified from Cambridge where she had managed to get enrolled in Newnham College, an adjunct of Cambridge University. Jane was surprised as she had heard that Girton College which was opened in 1870 was the only ladies college available to women and that had faded because it was not recognised by the university authorities. She had been furious at the time and had petitioned, together with Emmeline Pankhurst's mother, Sophie Goulden, to change it. She well remembered something that Queen Victoria was reported to have said, and which for decades women's progress in British society was haunted: Let women be what God intended, a helpmate for man, but with totally different duties and vocations.

"I did not realise that women's aspirations had advanced so far Miss…?"

"Susan Hastings, Madam. It is a shame really as we have to ask permission to attend classes and although we may qualify we are not permitted to get our degree, as are the men." She coloured up realising how vehemently she had uttered those words.

"My apologies, Madam, it does rankle somewhat."

"No apology necessary, Susan, I completely concur." Jane replied, heatedly.

Charles realised that they had reached a point where further interviews would be superfluous, Jane had already decided. To cap it all he recalled that it was also a 'Susan', her one time personal maid and now close friend, who had once saved Jane's life when she was wasting away because she believed him lost at sea – they had become good friends who still enjoyed contact from time to time.

They continued interviewing several other applicants in a somewhat desultory manner until Charles called a halt. He delegated the writing of the acceptance letter to Jane. Miss Susan

Hastings started the following Monday when her duties were outlined to her and she was introduced to her pupils, to whom she took an instant liking, and they to her.

With the departure of their nanny the games room had been converted into a school room, complete with a blackboard and all the necessary equipment with which to pursue their education. Susan soon became a friend and confidant to the two children whom she adored. She soon realised that the natural competition between the two obviated any pressure to apply themselves to their lessons and as such she found her job rewarding and pleasant; her love for the children grew daily.

The following Thursday a post office messenger arrived at Fordingbridge Hall with a message informing Lord Cholmondeley that a large parcel awaited him at Southampton's main post office. Without delay he had one of the grooms prepare the phaeton and had himself driven into town where he was delighted to take possession of a very large package – he was impatient to get back to the 'Hall' where he retired into his study to open it.

Several weeks previously he had read an article in the Devon and Exeter Gazette which appeared in print in 1902, wherein it had lauded Winston Churchill's military history by describing his pastime of playing war games with a magnificent collection of miniature soldiers comprising of many regiments and of many nations. It also, incidentally, mentioned that H.G. Wells had indulged in the same practice. The article included an old photograph depicting Churchill at age seven indulging his passion with soldiers lined up in a mock-up of the battle of Waterloo. It was reported that Winston's father, Lord Randolph Churchill, watched his son playing and asked him if he would like to join the army. These words had apparently changed his life.

It was also reported that an English firm, 'William Britains', were manufacturing a far better quality and less expensive line of hollow cast lead figures, about two and a half inches tall, depicting soldiers of many nations, all in authentic colours. Charles had ordered nearly 1000, representing soldiers of many nations, mostly European, and he was impatient to unpack them; however he bided his time until the afternoon lessons had finished and then he sent his footman to request the presence of his son. He arrived with his sister in tow a few minutes later.

As soon as Katie discovered what was in the parcel she left with a disdainful toss of her head to pursue more interesting occupations.

Christopher was as enthralled as his father as box sets of soldiers were unearthed from their wrappings and line after line of various regiments were displayed. The artillery regiments came complete with their artillery pieces and the Scots were in full regalia, complete with dirk and some with bagpipes. He was enthralled. That evening, Charles asked Jane if she knew where that chap was who used to do a lot of work for her – he had virtually rebuilt the parade room where she had initiated her first haute couture showing in one of her garment factories. "Oh! You are referring to Bill Bailey and his son?"

"Yes, that's the chappie. Do you know how to contact him?"

"Yes! Of course, I still use him from time to time. If you recall he moved his business to Southampton because of the plethora of work in this area."

"That's right. I also recall that it was you who found him that work;" he laughed.

"Would you please contact him and tell him that I have work for him?"

She tipped her head down and peered up at him from under her long eyelashes – which she was well aware aroused his passions, which invariably succeeded getting his acquiescence.

"Am I allowed to know what you want him for?"

"Stop doing that, you witch;" he smiled. "It will not work this time – you will find out in due course."

A few weeks later Susan became aware that Christopher was not concentrating on his work, which was not at all like him. She asked him if he had a problem, noticing his high colour and general lethargy.

"I am so sorry, Miss Susan, but I am not feeling all that well."

"He has been like that since yesterday," stated Catherine accusingly, "I tried to get him to tell mama, but just like a typical boy he would not admit to feeling ill. Boys!" she declared, rolling her eyes.

Susan directed him to his bed immediately - much against his wishes – as she hurried to find his mother, who she found tending flowers in the conservatory.

"I am so sorry to bother you, Madam, but I feel it incumbent upon me to inform you that I believe that Master Christopher is feeling unwell and I have taken the liberty of sending him to his bed."

Jane looked up from what she was doing, her face reflecting her concern.

"Thank you, Susan, I will go to him and see for myself."

On arrival at her son's bedroom she discovered that he had changed into his pyjamas and put himself into bed – which was a sure indication to her that he had accepted the fact that he was not well.

She placed her hand on his brow and was appalled to find it hot, she asked him to open his mouth and discovered that his throat was red and swollen.

"How long has it been like this, darling?"

He smiled weakly. "It came on suddenly yesterday, Mama," as he lay back wearily onto his pillow.

Jane suspected that this was the first indications of the dreaded influenza that had been sweeping the poorer districts of London and other major cities. Her knowledge was sketchy but she recalled that hundreds had died – without hesitation she called for Benson and directed him to send a groom to collect the local doctor, a Scotsman, Angus McPherson who arrived with a nurse.

"I hope ye dinna mind, my Lady, but if it is the flu that is doing the rounds he'll need constant attention. Unfortunately we have no cure for this at the moment, but he looks a strong lad and we must do all we can to help his own immune system to fight it. Ye'll ken that it won't be easy. The nurse will ensure that he gets plenty of fluids and will bathe him with cold water. She will send for me if he doesna respond."

All that day and night the nurse was in constant attendance, as was his mother who watched as her beloved son sank inexorably into a coma, from where it was feared he would not recover. Several times Katie appeared at the bedroom door pleading to be allowed to see her brother. Her mother fearing that she would also succumb to the same malady refused to let her near her brother.

"He needs me, Mother, please let me go to him."

Jane ached for her daughter, knowing of the bond between them, but fear of the consequences drove her.

She had two cots brought into the room for the nurse and herself; she took over attending her son when the nurse from necessity had to leave to eat and attend her personal needs. Resting on her cot Jane eventually, despite all her efforts fell into a deep sleep. Awaking some two hours later she discovered the exhausted nurse asleep on her cot and panicking, hurried to her son's bedside to find Katie snuggled in beside her brother; she looked so serene that she was loath to remove her and sought her husband's advice.

"It is rather pointless removing her now, Jane. If she is going to catch it she will already have done so."

As a precaution they again sent for Dr McPherson who began to berate his nurse for allowing Katie to get too close to his patient, Jane defended her.

"The poor girl was exhausted, Doctor; and I am just as culpable – what is done, is done and we have to hope for the best." The doctor grunted as he made his way to the bed to check his patient. He checked Katie first to see if she was showing any influenza symptoms, then he checked his patient.

"Well! I am pleased to say that the wee lassie doesna appear to have been infected but you should remove her at once."

Her mother reached for her daughter with the intention of removing her from where she was entwined with her brother. Katie looked at her with an uncompromising stare as she tightened her arms around her brother.

"No!" she snapped.

"Please, darling, it is for the best."

"No!"

Jane looked towards her husband for support. He was also well aware of the bond between his children. He shrugged helplessly.

"Leave them be Jane, it would be rather pointless now."

The doctor shook his head in disbelief.

"On yere heid be it then." As he stalked off.

Jane went about her duties with a heavy heart and noticed that all the servants that she came across during the morning were not wearing shoes; most had wool socks covering their feet. She turned to Benson.

"Benson! What is the meaning of this – the servants are not wearing shoes; is there a problem?"

Benson turned to face her; his wet eyes reflecting his deep concern.

"The only problem, Madam, is the young master's sickness – they all feel it acutely; they have removed their boots as a mark of respect, Madam; they thought that the noise of boots may disturb Master Christopher."

Jane turned away to hide her tears.

All of the previous day as Christopher had sunk into a coma his parents had despaired; going so far as to entreat the vicar at the local church to initiate prayers for his recovery, which all the servants who could be spared had attended; an air of desperate gloom settled over Fordingbridge Hall.

The doctor returned later that evening quite expecting to find his patient dead; he was surprised to find him still unconscious but alive. As before he checked Katie first, he took his time. He stood with a puzzled look on his face. Walking around to the other side of the bed he spent some time checking Christopher; repeating the procedure again he looked askance at the parents; who became agitated at his furrowed brow.

"What is it doctor?" Jane cried as Charles wrapped his arms around her.

The doctor looked at them for a long moment before replying.

"I confess to being totally bemused, Madam - Sir," he finally remarked. "The lassie is under great stress and is weak, but healthy – and the laddie appears to be stronger and has every chance of recovery. If I didna know better I would hazard a guess that the laddie is drawing strength from his sister – but of course that is impossible."

Just then Katie pulled away from her brother and with a deep sigh and laid back on her pillow. Christopher, for the first time in two days, opened his eyes and gave his sister a weak smile.

"Thank you, Poppet." He closed his eyes and went back to sleep.

All the trauma of that week had been kept from both grandmothers who enjoyed their isolation in quarters in the west wing of Fordingbridge Hall; when they finally discovered that one of their grandchildren had been desperately ill they were furious at Jane and Charles for not informing them. It had been deliberate on Jane's part as she was well aware that she could not possibly have coped with the two women's anguish and concern on top of her own distress.

They made amends by organising a picnic in the rose garden to which they invited the manager of Sinclair Farm, Jason, and his wife, Susan, and her daughter, Mary, who was three weeks older than Catherine. In addition, Susan, their tutor was also invited to attend, in order to become acquainted with other members of the family and their friends.

Susan had been Jane's maid in previous years and had married Jason, one of the estate managers. Jane's mother, Matilda, finding herself overstretched at the death of her husband, Jane's father, was happy to offer him the job as manager of the farm with Charles' agreement. Jason had been delighted to be appointed manager of the farm – and even more appreciative of the house that came with it in which to house his new wife; and eventually his daughter.

Charles stood to one side holding a tankard of the local cider as he gazed with appreciation at the three ladies sitting on the grass under an enormous beech tree. His wife, whom he adored; Susan, the Sinclair Farm manager's wife, a sonsy woman and dear friend who had once saved Jane's life, and Susan, the new tutor who Jane was introducing. Susan's daughter, Mary, was playing happily with his children; he managed to catch his wife's eye and signalled that he wished to speak with her. Jane excused herself from the group, wondering what Charles could want that could not wait.

"You wanted to speak with me, darling," she asked.

"Yes, Jane. I was wondering, as you have the two Susan's with you, if you had considered asking Jason's Susan if she would like to have her daughter, Mary, tutored with our two? Just a suggestion," he said with a smile.

"Thank you, Charles; I was contemplating asking you the same thing."

"Hmm, Perhaps we have the same rapport as our children," he laughed.

When Jane broached the subject both Susan's were delighted.

Jane looked at her friend, a question on her lips. "You realise that the farm is too far to travel every day, she would have to live in and you would only see her at weekends?"

Susan lowered her head for a while in silent contemplation, already feeling the daily loss of her daughter. Then she recognised the tremendous advantages of having her child properly educated and the benefits of her living in grace and luxurious surroundings and she choked back a sob as she thanked Jane for her offer. All three hugged, as women tend to do.

CHAPTER FOUR

Bill Bailey and his son arrived a week later.

"I am so sorry for the delay, my Lady", he said with a smile. They were old friends and Bill Bailey had completed many jobs for Jane when she was simply, Jane Sinclair – the owner of two very successful garment factories.

"I had to convert the toilets for Lord Branston – and thank you, Madam, for getting me that job."

"That is quite alright, Bill, my husband, Lord Chumley, has some work for you – you will find him in his study – you know the way; and how are you, Joe?" She said; directing her question towards Bill's son.

"Oim roit, thank you, my Lady; we 'eard that your son was very sick with the influenza and we said a prayer for 'im last Sunday week." He twisted his cap in his hands, embarrassed at his boldness.

"Thank you both, luckily your prayers were answered and he is recovering well." She carried on with her flower arranging as the two walked off.

Charles showed the baileys the boxes of toys and explained what he wanted. With the toy soldiers had been included a book with the ground plans of many famous battles together with battle tactics and a list of weaponry. Bill Bailey took one look at it and commented that he had seen a similar arrangement in one of the stately houses he had worked in, explaining that it had removable trees and buildings; bridges and landmarks. Charles was delighted and loaned him the book on which to base his work.

"I am sorry to tell you, Sir, that this job will take several weeks, Joe here is quite good at making the moveables and I'll concentrate on the main battleground. I have already been thinking about what I would do, if I had to do it, you understand, Sir, and I can certainly improve on the one I saw. I'm afraid I can't set a time, Sir, having not tried this sort of thing before."

"It will be alright Bill, take your time; Lady Jane speaks highly of you."

The Bailey's left discussing their ideas.

Three weeks later an old brewer's dray rumbled up the sweep of the driveway with a very large cloth wrapped board in the back. One of the footmen assisted the Baileys in getting it to the room especially prepared for it; there were a dozen boxes containing beautifully fashioned miniatures of trees, bridges, houses and a whole miscellany of carved pieces. The main board came complete with trestles and a baize cover. It was irregularly shaped and had provision for additions to be fitted in order to expand its use. Charles was very pleased and insisted on giving the Bailies an additional ten pounds above their account of twenty seven pounds. They set the board up and set all the accessories on the shelves arranged around the walls. He could not wait to show it to his son and sent a servant to Susan in the classroom to fetch him. He arrived a few minutes later and was equally delighted as his father. Using the book as a guide they began setting out the battle of Waterloo complete with all the topography and the soldiers in their authentic costumes. Over the following weeks whilst still concentrating on the Battle of Waterloo they reset the battlefield as best they could using the book which had come with the pieces. They discovered that the battle had been fought on Sunday 18th June 1815 on the border of the United Kingdom of the Netherlands. A French army under the command of Napoleon Bonaparte was defeated by the two armies of the Seventh Coalition; an Anglo led Allied army under the command of the Duke of Wellington, and a Prussian army under the command of Gebherd Leberecht von Blucher; Prince of Wahlstatt. Apparently Wellington and Blucher's armies were cantoned close to the north-eastern border of France. Napoleon chose to attack them in the hope of destroying them before they could join in a coordinated invasion of France with other members of the coalition.

Christopher and his father spent many happy evenings setting out the battlefield as best they could. At one time Charles had to send for Bill bailey to get him to make several bunkers and a few other details – all of which held up proceedings.

Christopher was reading from the book whilst his father set the pieces as described.

> "The French army under the command of Napoleon Bonaparte consisted of 73,000 men and the coalition of the armies of Britain; Netherlands; Hanover; Nassau; Brunswick and Russia could boast 118,000 men.

Napoleon sent a third of his forces to pursue the Prussians, who had withdrawn parallel to Wellington. This resulted in the separate and simultaneous Battle of Wavre with the Prussian rear-guard.

Upon learning that the Prussian army was able to support him, Wellington decided to offer battle on the Mont-Saint-Jean escarpment, across the Brussels road. Here he withstood repeated attacks by the French throughout the afternoon, aided by the progressively arriving Prussians.

In the evening Napoleon committed his last reserves in a desperate final attack, which was narrowly beaten back. With the Prussians breaking through on the French right flank, Wellington's Anglo-allied army counter-attacked in the centre, and the French army was routed."

The two of them were totally involved but Charles was peeved when he discovered that he had omitted to order neither Nassau nor Brunswick soldiers; he sent an urgent despatch to London to correct his error.

Finally the battlefield was set and the battle joined. They were so absorbed that neither was aware that Jane and Catherine had joined them and were watching the proceedings with unfeigned interest.

> "It is a beautiful sight," murmured, Jane. "But I do hope that you both think on the casualties of that battle; there were over 65,000 men killed or wounded, it must surely convince you both of the futility of war"

Charles looked up in surprise. "Hello, darling, I am impressed with your knowledge'" he smiled. "Why would you know that?" he enquired.

Jane hugged Catherine to her as they both laughed.
"We have been sneaking in here when you have both been elsewhere and have read the book – and, incidentally, I think you have made an error." She reached out and picking up a bridge moved it to a slightly different position. "There! That's better," she stated with a gloating smile on her face.

By the time that the third battle was reached Christopher was beginning to notice flaws in the strategies and conduct of the main protagonists and suggesting alternative actions - his father encouraged him in his efforts to improve the conduct of the battles. He was particularly impressed when his son remarked that frontal battle made no sense in many respects and that in the future battles would be won by ambushes and stealth; tactics used by the Boers in the Transvaal in 1880. In the months that followed they processed the Battle of Vienna in 1529; the Battle of Cajamarca in 1532, where Francisco Pizarro conquered the largest amount of territory ever taken in a single battle and on to The Battle of Antietam in the American Civil War of 1862 which was the bloodiest day in American history.

Whilst Catherine was interested in the war games enacted by her brother and her father she had no inclination to join them. However, one day, whilst beguiling her father in his study she remarked on the set of duelling swords that were mounted above the fireplace.

> "Ah, father! These swords are a beautiful decoration but they do have unpleasant connotations, do they not? Did you ever fight a duel?"
>
> "Certainly not Katie; duelling died out many years ago, I believe the last duel fought in England was in 1850 something. However I was considered fairly competent in the noble art of fencing in my younger days," he smiled.
> "Will you teach me how to fence?"
>
> "Certainly not," he repeated, "it is not a woman's sport."

Looking up at him from her lowered head, she peered up from beneath her long eyelashes.

"Please, father, I could practice with Christopher." She pleaded.

"I see that you have acquired your mother's coquetry in order to get your own way," he laughed. "I really do not have suitable protective clothing – I suppose my old gear would fit Christopher," he mused.

"My friend, Dianne, Lord Tewksbury's daughter has joined a fencing club in London – She will know where to get the right clothing."

Charles, knowing when he was beaten agreed and a month later tuition began. Charles, slightly overweight found the exercise rewarding, however within two months he was having great difficulty in holding his own. Katie and Christopher practiced most days and in spite of his superior height and strength Christopher found himself struggling to hold his own against his sister, who on many weekends joined her friend, Dianne in specialised training with her fencing master who arrived from London for her lessons. She discovered, from him, that Angelo's School of Arms, in Carlisle House, Soho, had been formed in 1763 and was still going strong. They found most of the French terms easy to remember as both spoke the language fairly competently; Appel; Allez; Attaque au fer; croise and many other directions. She discovered that fencing had been part of the Olympics Games in the summer of 1896. Sabre events had been held at every Summer Olympics as had foil and Epee. Catherine progressed so well that Dianne's fencing master suggested that she join the English Olympic fencing team – much to Dianne's chagrin and Christopher's delight.

Their tuition progressed rapidly under Susan's guidance and being well aware of her charges aspirations she concentrated on the Oxford entrance examination curriculum. She had collected several past papers and worked out the subjects most likely to be listed and concentrated on those; although she insisted (as she put it) on a well rounded education. Catherine had decided on a medical career; Susan suspected that this would put her charge in a position where she could use her influence to change the system. She was well aware that Catherine had already contacted Amelia Pankhurst, who was now almost sixty, protesting over an education system tailored to the requirements of men to the detriment of women; she also recalled being told by Lady Jane about her various issues when she had invoked the assistance of Amelia's mother, Mrs Goulden over working conditions for her workers when she owned two garment factories.

CHAPTER FIVE

Several years passed with Christopher and Catherine competing for an advantage at every opportunity. Mary was bright but could not match the brilliance of the other two.

"I do not mind at all, Katie," she smiled. "You and Chris are destined for great things, and I wish you joy, but my ambitions only go as far as marrying a fine farmer and having children," she blushed slightly at this. "I am very fortunate in having this opportunity to acquire a good education and to moderate my speech – both of these will undoubtedly assist me in finding a good husband and drawing the best out of life. For that I am deeply grateful; in addition to that I have acquired the two best friends a girl could have – and," she added, "two sets of wonderful parents."

Jane sat in the arboretum pulling on a pair of stout walking boots, her hair was pulled back and tied with a ribbon. She stood up and smoothed her skirt, which was a favourite of her husband. They had decided to walk to his secret place – the thought sent a shiver of anticipation through her body. It was a place where he used to hide from his father's wrath when he was a young lad; he had shown her the place when they were courting; it was where he had proposed to her and it was where subsequently they invariably made love on the moss covered rock, secure in their isolation.

She turned as a footman arrived bearing a letter addressed to her. She was surprised to recognise the beautiful free script of Abe Snape who had been the manager of one of her factories and who had subsequently bought it. Breaking the seal she read.

Dear Lady Cholmondelay. Jane, if I may be so bold.

There are rumblings abroad that can no longer be ignored; events are evolving that may affect our interests. I have appreciated that you have long had your finger on the pulse of international events pertinent to our business. If it is not too much of an imposition I would be grateful if you would acquaint me with your opinion as to our best course of action.

I would further be delighted to see you and your charming husband and to see your children who am assured are a delight. I do realise that it has been some time since you divested yourself of your businesses and that you may not be so au fait with international events – however, having some knowledge of your diligence I am sure that my visit will be profitable financially and personally.

Yours sincerely.
Abe Snape.

Jane read the letter several time with Charles, who had just arrived, reading it over her shoulder.

"Oh, Charles, I have been so remiss; for several years I have been benefitting from my shares in both companies and I have contributed nothing. I really do not think that I am fully conversant with international affairs as I once was. How can I advise Abe?"

"Well, Jane. It will be several weeks before he arrives and that will give you time to reacquaint yourself with pertinent details."

"We must postpone our walk until later. I must write a reply for the messenger." She rang the bell for Benson.

"Benson. Please take care of this messenger and see that he is refreshed, he has a long ride ahead of him."

Abe Snape arrived ten days later.

The day prior to his arrival, Katie, who had been taking cooking lessons from the cook decided that she would produce cakes to add to the celebrations. Her brother, who was somewhat sceptical of her prowess as a chef, but keen to encourage her, took one as they cooled from the oven. Katie watched him assessing his reaction.

"Mmm," he mumbled as he headed for the back door where he surreptitiously spat the cake out hoping that Max, the dog, would finish it off. Max took one sniff and walked off disdainfully, much to Christopher's embarrassment. Katie, passing the window, happened to see both her brother's reaction and, worst of all, the dog's scornful rejection. She checked her ingredients carefully and realised that she had used salt instead of sugar, she was mortified.

Luckily her sense of humour rose to the fore; however, that afternoon she inveigled him into several bouts of fencing with the two artillery swords that had adorned her father's study wall and pushed her attack with such vigour that she thrashed him four bouts in a row.

After a very successful early dinner where Jane introduced Abe to her children and their tutor, they all retired to the parlour where her husband, Christopher, Katie and their tutor were given the option of retiring to their own devices or join in the conversation; which they all knew would be Jane's assessment of the political situation as it applied to the possibility of war and its effects on the garment factories which she had once owned. All chose to stay. They settled themselves comfortably, some choosing tea and some trying the new coffee, which had recently been imported and was becoming popular in the more 'up market' cafes in London. Jane addressed the group.

"As you all are well aware Germany has for some time been building up its naval power; this is obviously a potential threat to our Royal Navy which has for many years been superior and a bulwark against aggression. This is well appreciated by our government who have entered into an Entente Cordial with France and there are rumours that an alliance with Russia is in the offing. This build up is obviously for a reason. There are also rumours that the Germans are forming alliances – this leads me inevitably towards the view that it needs only a comparatively small event to push Germany over the edge in provoking a war." Turning to Abe she looked askance; he nodded.

"If you would, Jane; how will this affect our business?
– I do have some ideas."

"I am sure that you have, Abe. If I were you I would be hoarding all the material that you can find; there will be shortages. I would also concentrate your output on military uniforms and, as this war will inevitably involve more women, concentrate on those garments suitable for women – nurses, doctors, etcetera. There will also be women replacing men in factories and industry; they will want protective clothing, safety boots, aprons and caps or snoods. There will also be a great need for bandages and slings, sheets and blankets – all those things incumbent on wars. I suggest you contact the procurer for army equipment and get the designs and the medical hierarchy for uniform types; the expansion of our military and ancillary organisations will be enormous. You should also be aware that camouflage khaki has replaced the traditional dress uniforms, much against the wishes of the officer class," she smiled, "so it would be sensible to buy up as much of that material as possible." She paused and looked around. "I should also mention that our navy will also be expanding so blue serge will be in demand.

It is estimated that we will have just 250,000 men if the war started tomorrow but there can be no doubt that this number will treble as the need for more men increases. Many regiments will expand and some regiments will merge. It would be to your advantage if you found somebody like David Lloyd George's secretary to cultivate, he of course has superseded Kitchener as war lord. I am afraid, Abe, it is not a matter of what you know but who you know. All industries will increasingly depend on industrial spying, paying people to ferret out secrets. It won't be nice but it is the way of the world these days," she sighed.

Abe looked up from his scribbling. "Thank you, Jane, that was very enlightening, I have already cornered as much of the market as possible on some items such as buttons and insignia. I have also suggested to Claude Duval that he expand his business and concentrate on army boots."

Jane recalled that Claude Duval had produced the specialised shoes and novelty boots for her ladies to wear in her haute couture shows.

Jane smiled. "I would have thought that Claude would have retired by now."

"No, Jane. He is just as outrageous as ever; I really do not know from where he derives his energy. He must be well into his sixtieth year by now," he smiled.

Jane paused as she remembered Claude Duval her one time friend and bootmaker for her haute couture shows. She recalled that the Frenchman had a humped back that did nothing to dampen his outrageous humour, his violin playing and his risqué comments that had delighted her clientele.

"I am so pleased that he is still with us; do give him my fond regards when you see him."

Abe rose to his feet. "Thank you, Jane, for your advice; it was very enlightening, as usual. But I must leave you now and return to London and utilise your information." Jane clung to him for a long moment as she recalled their long association and of his many kindnesses to her when she had taken over a run-down garment factory. She hugged him as tears rimmed her eyes.

He took his departure for Southampton to catch a train connection to London.

CHAPTER SIX

Charles and Christopher continued with their battle reconstructions which had progressed into a somewhat different field where they tried to improve on the tactics used in various battles. Charles had been reading of a relatively new invention of a machine gun that had been invented by Hiram Maxim that bore his name. The original version was invented in 1884 and was first offered to the British army; unfortunately the British High Command rejected it in spite of estimates that the gun had a fire power equivalent to as many as sixty to one hundred rifles; some British officers even regarded the weapon as an improper form of warfare. The Germans adopted the weapon with great delight purchasing some twelve thousand.

Charles was fuming as he told Christopher of the stupidity of the British High Command.

"If the indications are correct we will probably be at war with the Bosch quite soon and because of our army's outdated thinking our men will be slaughtered by this weapon" Christopher entirely agreed.

On July 23, Austria-Hungary presented an ultimatum to Serbia. Vienna, however, intentionally imposing impossible demands to Serbia in order to be able to declare war on its neighbour for 'orchestrating' the assassination of Archduke Franz Ferdinand of Austria. A few days later, the Austro-Hungarian troops invaded Serbia and started the devastating World War.

On 4 August 1914, Britain (and its Empire) entered the war. Britain's reasons for declaring war were complex: the Treaty of London of 1839 had committed it to safeguard Belgium's neutrality, and the strategic risk posed by German control of the Belgian coast was unacceptable. Asquith proceeded to form a new coalition government on 25 May, with the majority of the new cabinet coming from his own Liberal party and the Unionist (Conservative) party brought in to shore up the government. By January 1915, 184 members of parliament were serving with the armed forces.

Charles was concerned when conscription was introduced and he started to lose men from the estate; labourers who worked the fields, even overseers, and soon after he was getting requests from the staff to leave and join one of the services. He argued that the nation would want the food that they grew, but in many cases the men had no choice. He realised that the days of large numbers of servants was past and that he would have to do with the women and the infirm. He adjusted and managed as best he could. A month into the war casualties began to arrive back in England from France and the hospitals were swamped, especially so after the battle of Ypres – which the troops referred to as Wipers - on October 18th. In desperation the authorities scouted the land for places in which to set up temporary hospitals. Charles immediately offered the large ballroom in the 'Hall'. A few days' later trucks arrived bearing beds and linen and all those things necessary for the care of the wounded.

Christopher missed his sister; Catherine had passed the Cambridge University entrance exam eighteen months previously – well before the normal age because of her entry results which had been near perfect. She had enrolled in the faculty of medicine with the clear intention of qualifying as a doctor; a profession in which she was eminently suitable. Her time off was spent looking after the wounded in the ballroom where over eighty officers were being treated for a miscellany of wounds. Catherine was appalled when she saw all those fine men, some crippled for life and some cruelly disfigured. There was some confusion when she first started treating their wounds, but her laughing comment that Florence Nightingale had been more than accepted soon had them smiling; most of them could not get enough of her treatment and truth be known many fell head over heels with the beautiful trainee.

Catherine went about her duties with a barely subdued anger at the treatment of women and the difficulties placed in the path of women who craved education. It was still very difficult for her to get a university education, although men had no such restriction. Her mother had told her of her own frustrations at the limitations placed on women's education and of the time when Emily Davies and Barbara Bodichon had set up a college for women in 1870 but it had failed due to it not being recognised by the university authorities. In 1880 Newnham College was established at Cambridge University and by 1910 there were just over a thousand women students at Oxford and Cambridge. However, she had to obtain permission to attend lectures and she was not allowed to take her degree.

Without a university degree it was very difficult for women to enter the profession. After a long struggle the medical profession had allowed women to become doctors. Even so, by 1900 there were only a comparatively few women qualified. She suspected that a war, as bad as that would be, would inevitably give a great impetus to women's acceptance in all branches of the workforce.

She spent all of her spare time, and there was precious little of that, expanding her medical knowledge, she realised that to be considered the equal of men in the profession she would have to be twice as knowledgeable. She was fortunate in that she became close friends with a young surgeon who invited her to attend his operations – and even surreptitiously to assist him. She was extremely grateful as had he been discovered he would have undoubtedly been dismissed; truth to tell he was madly in love with her and was happy to take the risk to help her.

Christopher at the age of seventeen was tall for his age, broad shouldered and fit and he chaffed at the bit, anxious to get into the war before it finished. Most politicians were of the opinion that the war would be over within the year and he wanted to do his bit to end it. On August the 23rd Germany invaded France and the British Expeditionary Force was forced to withdraw from Mons with great loss of life. He discussed the situation with his father.

His father studied his son, whom he loved dearly. He understood his impatience to get into the war but his overpowering wish was to keep him out of it.

> "Christopher, my son. You realise that conscription is for men between the ages of eighteen to forty, you are only seventeen."

> "Sir! There are many men who have joined up at seventeen and I feel like a coward not being in it. I do not want glory, but I do want the servants and my friends to know that I am prepared to go to war as indeed many of our workers have. Apart from which, father, I would die of shame if I received a white feather"

> "Christopher, I fully understand your problem but I sincerely believe that Admiral Sir Charles Fitzgerald did a shameful thing when he initiated the white feather to indicate cowardness. Many men have very important jobs to do that help the war effort. Apart from which it is easy for women or those sitting behind a desk to accuse others of being cowards. The organisation of the white feather does not discriminate

between those whose input helps us win the war, and those with disabilities who could not cope with war conditions. Even our wounded soldiers in mufti have been given them; it is shameful;" he went on to add. "It is not possible to purchase a commission these days, Christopher; that was abolished in 1871 as part of the Cardwell Reforms; at one time you could become a captain in the Life Guards for 3,500 pounds."

Christopher erupted. "I can assure you, Sir, that I would never consider that avenue. I would intend to earn my commission."

"Well, son; I understand your wish to enlist but I doubt if your mother would. If you did join up which regiment would you consider?"

"The same as many of our workers have joined, the Hampshires; I may even meet up with them," he smiled.

"Should I agree to this – and I would have an almighty tussle with your mother - I should remind you that there is nothing noble about war. It is mainly a case of waiting around, hunger, discomfort and disease; and that is before you get to fight."

"I have no illusions, Sir."

Charles was in a quandary; he knew if he sanctioned Christopher's wish to join the army he would have a mighty battle on his hands with Jane when she discovered what he had done; on the other hand he understood his son's eagerness to help his country defeat the Huns. He had the same urgings but at the age of forty-seven he knew he was too old for active service; instead he used his considerable organisational skills to run the administration of the hospital and to organising the distribution of food that the estate grew.

Charles' and Jane's mothers had died within a week of each other just over four years previously and there had been a double funeral which was widely attended – that had left the west wing of Fordingbridge Hall available for the hospital staff's accommodation and administration.

He wandered out to the conservatory where he knew Jane would be; she spent most of her time growing and potting the beautiful flowers that decorated the hospital and the nurse's rooms. He stood in the doorway and let his eyes absorb her. To him she was just as beautiful at forty-six as she was when he first met her picking blackberries in the New Forest when she was just sixteen. Her hair was slowly turning grey and her body was slightly more rounded; he still loved her with the same passion. She sensed his presence and straightened slowly.

"Hello, darling! I was just thinking of you," she smiled.

"Snap!" he laughed. "I was just thinking of you." He pulled her to him and kissed the top of her head. Jane lifted her chin for the kiss that she knew would come.

"You first," she smiled.

Charles enlightened her with the talk he had with their son.

"Oh, dear!" She sighed. "Catherine finishes her studies next year and I know that she wants to go to France to treat the wounded there in the field hospitals. I sincerely hope that this damned war will be over before then."

Charles looked askance; it was the first time he had heard his wife swear in all the years that they had known each other.

Jane looked at him a worried frown creasing her brow.

"If the war finishes, as the politicians predict it will within the year, the children will be deeply disappointed that they will not be able to do their bit for king and country, but I really do not want them to go."

Charles smiled, "I assure you darling that there is absolutely no prospect of that happening. Let us tell them to wait – and in the meantime they can prepare themselves better in ways that will increase the chances of survival. If anything should deter them it is the sight of those poor souls we have in the ballroom."

Christopher and Jane were informed of their parent's point of view.

Christopher would not consider challenging his parent's decision. His studies at Oxford took up the greater portion of his time. He found the study of the law and all of its complexities enormously interesting, especially the tangled web of Tort; but in those moments when he had time he studied all of the aspects of war; he was currently revising the working details of the Maxim gun. He discovered that the Maxim machine gun, usually positioned on a flat tripod, would require a gun crew of four to six operators. In theory they could fire 400-600 small- caliber rounds per minute, with rounds fed via a fabric belt or a metal strip. Whether air or water cooled the machine guns still jammed frequently, especially in hot conditions or when used by inexperienced operators. He was reading from Jane's book on army weaponry. The company was formed in 1898 by Fred T James and was becoming a handbook of knowledge of ships and weapons, He spent many hours improving his knowledge of weapons and tactics – most of which he thought out of date.

He was convinced that the current trench warfare was ridiculous – as evinced by the plethora of casualties being brought back to England.

In designing his machine gun, Hiram Maxim utilized a simple concept. The gas produced by the explosion of powder in each machine gun cartridge created a recoil which served to continuously operate the machine gun mechanism. No external power was needed. His initial design, which was water cooled and belt fed, allowed for a theoretical rate of fire of up to 600 rounds per minute (half that number in practice). It was heavy however, weighing in at just over 136 lbs.

By the time he turned eighteen he was well advanced in his studies and had no problems about leaving them to enlist, as many others had before him.

With his father's reluctant sanction Christopher Cholmondelay applied to the army recruiting office in Winchester and signed on in the infantry where he was given a pamphlet that informed him that The Hampshire Regiment was formed on 1 July 1881 under the Childers reforms from the merger of the 37th (North Hampshire) Regiment of Foot and the 67th (South Hampshire) Regiment of Foot along with the militia and rifle volunteers of the county of Hampshire. He enlisted as a private.

A few days before he was required to report for duty his parents decided to give a party for Christopher and all the other men who had decided to enlist – or had been drafted. They splurged their limited resources on a feast that had not been seen in years, which culminated in dancing that got slightly out of hand due to the thought that this may be their last opportunity before they went to the front. The sadness of leaving Poppet clouded Christopher's enjoyment and he relished every moment alone with her.

As was common practice Christopher completed six weeks basic training on Salisbury Plain which had been used for that purpose since 1898. The 1st Battalion, 11th Brigade, 4th Division of which he was a recruit landed in Le Havre on August 23rd 1914. They had one day there whilst all of their equipment caught up with them and then entrained for Verdun-sur-Meuse. After what seemed to Christopher to be unnecessary confusion they were marched to the front line where two lines of trenches faced each other about two hundred yards apart. His platoon, together with many others, were to be held in reserve a few hundred yards to the rear of the front line. Christopher was appalled; the trenches had been hacked out of, what had once been a corn field in the middle of a shallow valley which had allowed the trenches to flood to a depth of approximately two feet. His platoon under the command of Sergeant Evan Evans was ordered to occupy the trench. Christopher could see another trench halfway up the hill which he knew were dry. He pointed this out to the sergeant.

"Ours is not to question why…"

"I am aware of Alfred Lord Tennyson's poem, sergeant, but why do we not move into the dry trenches. In this weather half the chaps will be dead before we see the enemy."

The sergeant was a large man of Welsh extraction. He was well aware who private Chumley was. Christopher had been gladdened to discover a charge hand from the Hall, Bertie Peters, had been allocated to the same platoon; Bertie had been equally pleased to see the son of Sir Charles Cholmondelay and evinced his surprise.

"What are you doing here, Sir?" he stammered; shouldn't you be with the officers, Sir? The rest of the platoon had gathered around, they were all wondering the same thing; his speech and general bearing set him aside from the rest, try as he might to fit in. Although only a private some of the men, without thinking, addressed him as, Sir. It soon became known that he was the son of Sir Charles Cholmondelay and without thinking they deferred to him.

The sergeant drew himself up to his full impressive height. He was in an invidious position; he was a good sergeant and well liked by his men but he had been in the army a long time and could tell an officer when he saw one; his natural caution told him not to antagonise somebody who may soon be his superior. In addition he had formed a loose friendship with Christopher who was constantly asking his sergeant to relate his experiences in various parts of the world.

"I am aware of who you are son," he said, "and I am also sergeant of this platoon so I outrank you. I am in agreement with you, but my boss, Lieutenant Toser has ordered us into those trenches and that is what we will do—if you want to argue with him, feel free to do so."

Christopher shrugged his shoulders and turned away intending to carry out the order when a despatch rider turned up skidding to a halt as he espied the sergeant.

"Hi, Sarg!" he called out, he obviously knew the man, "new orders from Division Headquarters." He handed over an envelope and with a cheerful wave was off.

The sergeant tore open the envelope and scanned the short note inside. He looked up unfolding a small map as he did so.

"A reprieve, lads. Apparently they are having a spot of bother along the road where the Germans have set up an ambush site – our orders are to winkle them out. So collect ya gear and watch ya step." They set off back along the road to the village of Dun-sur-Muese, which was close to the Argonne Forest. The sergeant stopped near the deserted outbuildings to consult the map that had arrived with his orders. "Only another mile, lads, the krauts have apparently set up an ambush among the trees, they have been shooting up anything of ours that moves – including two ambulances."

He set them into a skirmish formation and they advanced using the large trees and tangled undergrowth as cover. They had progressed about half a mile in this fashion when a burst of fire from among a rocky outcrop that overlooked the road slammed into the sergeant who was about ten paces ahead of his troop. The platoon immediately went to ground, seeking cover where they could. Chris, who had a great affection for the rough and tough sergeant could see where his boots jutted out from behind a large rock. Ignoring his own safety he crawled forward on his belly to go to the sergeant's assistance, ignoring the shots that peppered the rocks and trees around him. When he reached the sergeant's position he could see quite clearly that he was dead, a round had removed a part of his skull and several shots had hit him in the chest. He felt his anger rise. The war up to that point had been fairly remote; he had seen casualties being carried by stretcher bearers and plenty of blood. But this was a man who he had admired, he had eaten with him and shared a conversation or two and he had told them tales of various actions he had been in when serving in India and North Africa. He crawled back to where the rest of the men were, automatically taking charge.

"Who has any grenades on them?" Two men groped for them in their belts and handed them over.

"Right, chaps, we obviously can't stay here, they can pick us off at their leisure. We can't retire and we are pinned down. I want you to give me covering fire so that I can get near enough to lob these."

Bertie Peters piped up, "Don't do that, Sir, there has to be another way" – apart from anything else he was terrified at the thought of returning to Fordingbridge Hall and telling Chris' father that his son was dead.

"Chris growled, "If you can think of an alternative let me know. Right lads start firing," he yelled as he sprinted for the rocks ahead. There was crackling of rifles behind him as he reached a position where he could use the grenades. He pulled the pin from the first one and with his best bowling action tossed one into the position where the most fire was coming. He pulled the pin of another and tossed that to his left where another gun had opened up. He had just set himself to throw another when he felt a shocking blow high up on his left side spinning him around and pitching him to the ground. He saw a German soldier looming over him and resigned himself for the shot to come; then as the German was levelling his weapon he saw him suddenly spin away and he could hear the roar of the rest of his platoon as they finished off those Germans who were left. He passed out.

When he came to he saw that his friends had made a stretcher of poles stuck through the sleeves of their jackets and were carrying him back to their base, he sunk back into oblivion.

CHAPTER SEVEN

Catherine, who was helping a nurse with a patient suddenly stopped, her head raised in a listening attitude and with a cry ran from the ward to find her mother who was, as usual, in the conservatory talking to her husband. She threw herself at her mother sobbing and frantic.

"What is it, darling, whatever is wrong?" Her father, guessing her problem surrounded both of them with his arms. It was a few moments before she could speak.

"Oh. Mamma, it is Christopher, he has been wounded." She howled.

Both of her parents knew enough about their children's mental attachment not to question it. Her father released her.

"What else can you tell us, darling? He is not dead is he?"

"No. father I would know that," she sobbed, clinging to her mother.

"Well! I have some pull in that direction, I'll get the minister to find out where he is and what state he is in. We'll get him sent here and look after him ourselves."

Christopher regained consciousness and found himself in a forward field hospital. He awoke to find the men of his platoon queuing up to give blood. Not all was suitable but the staff took it anyway. Chris had lost a lot of blood since being shot and was very weak. He was fortunate in that blood group systems were just recently discovered by Karl Landsteiner in 1901 and had been adopted by army surgeons.

He tuned inwardly to his sister, Poppet, gaining strength as he did so – he strove to send a message to her that he was alright.

Captain Saunders of the regiment visited him the following day, praising his bravery in saving the men of his unit and with all due ceremony presented him with his Sergeant's stripes; which as Christopher knew was most unusual, that being a battlefield promotion (or field promotion) which is an advancement in military rank that occurs while deployed in combat. He was aware that a standard field promotion was advancement from current rank to the next higher rank; a 'jump-step' promotion is advancement from current rank to a rank above the next highest, which as he knew was very rare.

The Captain smiled at Chris' bemused expression. "Congratulations, Chumley, on your advancement; you are now in charge of your platoon. The general consensus among the staff is that you should be commissioned, partly because of your action in saving your platoon, but mainly because you should have taken a commission when you enlisted, as you were qualified to do – never mind, perhaps next time; if there is one, he shook his hand. Then as an afterthought he congratulated Chris again.

"By the way, you have been recommended for the Military Medal, it should come through in the next few days." He smiled as he patted the hand that rested on the sheet and took his leave.

Chris was slightly bemused by all that had happened to him in such a short time. He recalled when he was studying the award system current in the British armythat the Military Medal was awarded to other ranks and Commonwealth Forces. It was an award for gallantry and devotion to duty when under fire in battle on land. On the reverse of the medal is inscribed "For Bravery in the Field". Recipients of the medal are entitled to use the letters M.M. after their name. He was honoured to receive it, if indeed he did. He made good progress and was pleased when some men of his platoon came to visit and to congratulate him on his promotion. Chris was too embarrassed to inform them of his other award. That afternoon he was told that he would be repatriated back to England for three weeks convalescence – he hoped that it was to Fordingbridge Hall; which indeed it was; his father having had a hand in arranging it.

The ambulance drew up outside of the front of the house and Benson, who had been co-opted into helping with the war wounded, stepped forward to assist the soldier who was stepping gingerly down from the ambulance, Chris was still heavily bandaged and had his arm in a sling. Benson was slow to recognise him, but when he did he gave a loud bellow for the footman to call Lady Jane and Sir Charles, however before they arrived Catherine came racing from where she was working in the ballroom and with tears in her eyes helped him into the house – all was chaos as the entire staff rushed to see their favourite son.

The first week of his convalescence he slept a lot with his mother and Poppet fussing over him; but as he gradually gained strength he went for short walks with his sister which increased in duration daily. At the end of twelve days Catherine deemed his wound had healed enough to allow her to remove the dressings. By the time he was due to return to France he was fully recovered. He was pleased to meet up with his platoon which, short of a platoon commander had been allocated hospital duties – they were pleased to see him back. For the next four months they watched as other county regiments were decimated, in what Sergeant Chumley considered ridiculous trench warfare, as the Hampshire Regiment was held in reserve, until eventually the Hampshire's were sent to the front line. Christopher was appalled at the conditions that the men were expected to endure. Most of the trenches had at least a foot of mud topped with another foot of water; there were no duck boards to walk on to keep the men above the wet. He protested to his superior officer, lieutenant Knowles, known as Nobby behind his back.

"What do you expect me to do about it? Sergeant; anyway it won't be for long – we are ordered to go over the top tomorrow," he said, total resignation in his voice.

"That is suicide, Sir. The Germans have machine gun teams to the east and west, perfectly situated in an enfilading position; none of our men can get through. We have lost the Wiltshire regiment entirely and a large proportion of two other regiments."

"Well, sergeant we may be lucky this time." He went to turn away.

"You must be aware, sir, that those Maxims are each equivalent to about eighty rifles, with two of them crossing we don't have a chance."

"I am well aware of that, sergeant, but we have our orders." "Sir, what if we could wipe out those machineguns?"

"Yes, sergeant and what if pigs could fly," he scoffed dismissively. "Sir! If I could have four men I think I could do it."

"Well, sergeant, if you have a feasible plan you can explain it to the Captain – are you prepared to do that?" he said with a tinge of hope in his voice.

The sergeant shrugged his shoulders. "Well! We have to do something, Sir, we have lost most of the Wiltshire's and a large part of the East Sussex and to date not one man has broken through."

He was taken to the Company Commander, Captain Fielding who was drinking his tea in his tent, and the situation was explained to him.

He eyed the sergeant with some distain.

> "The only reason that I am listening to you is because of your father, Sir Charles. I don't normally take advice from a sergeant," he muttered with ill concealed venom; "and just how do you expect to do this, sergeant?" He placed emphasis on the rank.

Christopher tried hard to suppress his anger.

> "My intention is to get to the end of the Argonne Forest, Sir, and work our way west to the gun emplacement during the night."

> "You must be aware that that forest will be swarming with German troops, sergeant." He said with sneer.

> "I am aware of that and we will have to play it by ear, sir" He added as an afterthought.

> "I'll hold the attack for two days, that is all you get sergeant. Pick your men and get out."

As they wandered back to their lines the sergeant heard the lieutenant mutter sotto voce. "Arrogant pig!"

The men of the platoon realised that if they were ordered to attack the next morning their chances of survival were nil. He had no shortage of volunteers, especially as they held their new sergeant in high regard.

Chris chose his equipment carefully. He did not want the impact grenades as they had a nasty habit of exploding when a soldier went to ground in a hurry. He chose the timed type, which he knew was in short supply and which was handed out reluctantly; the Germans had no such shortage.

He managed to scrounge two for all of the five men and ensured that all of his men had filled their water bottles and had five hundred rounds each for their rifles – all ready in spare loading magazines. Private Bertie Peters proved to be an excellent scrounger – a highly valued person in any army- and produced four tins of corned beef and a packet of hard tack biscuits. As soon as the sergeant considered them as ready as they could be under the circumstances they set off walking eastward through devastated villages and past orchards which had been divested of all their fruit, until they could see a point of entry into the forest. Chris surveyed the area with his binoculars for a long minute but could see no Germans; they were about five miles from the front.

There was a long dry stone wall surrounding a field that stopped just short of the trees; bending low Chris led his men along the wall and into the tree line where they hid themselves as best they could in the thickets. Three hours passed as they waited for darkness; several times they could hear German voices as groups headed for the front lines; they made no effort to hide themselves believing the allies to be several miles away. At that time of the year it was never completely dark and the patrol worked their way westward to where the machine gun team was situated. Several times they had to make detours around German bivouacs.

Eventually they reached a point at the edge of the forest where they could make out the outlines of the machine gun nest in the early morning haze. The German crew were setting it up ready for the attack which they knew would come as daylight broke through the clouds. Chris took two more grenades from his men to add to his two. He briefed his men to hold their fire until he had managed to get close enough to lob his grenades. He began to crawl using broken tree stumps and broken walls in order to hide his approach. Twice he saw a helmeted head pop up but their gaze was always towards the English lines. He managed to get within twenty paces of the redoubt without being noticed; he estimated that there were five men in the emplacement. He pulled the pin from a grenade, holding the lever fully down, then rising to his feet he lobbed it into the gun emplacement; quickly arming another he tossed it into the gun mechanism putting it out of action. By now the German front line some eighty feet away had become aware of his presence and were firing at him. The fire was being returned by his men as they furiously worked the loading mechanism of their .303 Lee-Enfield rifles. They were yelling for him to get back. Chris was dropping to cover when a bullet struck him in the side of the head; his men could see the spurt of blood as their sergeant fell. They were sure he was dead. They retired, sick at heart.

It was a while before the Germans sent a replacement team and some time before they had removed the mangled machinegun and then started to remove the bodies; that is when they discovered that the English sergeant who had led the attack was not dead but critically wounded. Several of the German soldiers were all for finishing him off, however one, noting his tender age, suggested that they take him back to their lines hoping to get some information from him.

"He'll never make it Carl, let's finish him off, it will be quite an effort to get him back and by the look of him he won't make it." But Carl and another soldier took him by the arms and keeping his head free of the rough terrain dragged him back to their lines and into the first aid station about a hundred yards from the front line trenches. The German surgeon examined him and directed them to place him under the shade of a long veranda alongside many others; exclaiming that he had many more German soldiers to deal with that had a greater chance to survive. The German soldiers shrugged their shoulders and rejoined their comrades.

During this time his sister had completed four years of her doctors training and with the experience gained in the operating theatre, with the assistance of her friend doctor Martin, was well qualified, although much to her chagrin she was not awarded her certificate. She immediately volunteered as an army doctor and was sent to a field hospital located about twenty miles from the front; where she agitated to be allowed to go to the forward medical field hospital – a request that was constantly denied.

Katie was working in the field hospital and was setting splints and bandaging a wounded soldier's broken arm when she experienced the same feeling as on other occasions when something had happened to her brother. She clenched her teeth as she continued what she was doing; then ensuring that her patient was comfortable she hurried to the administrative office asking for time off for a personal matter. She had to listen to a long lecture as to the needs of her patients and of the shortage of doctors and of priorities, but eventually he appraised her with a smile.

"I take it, doctor, that this personal matter is important enough to drag you away from your patients? I have no problem with your dedication to our wounded, in fact I was going to suggest you take a break. I do hope that this personal matter will allow you some time to rest – you may have five days; and good luck with whatever it is that you have to do." He smiled as he dismissed her.

Katie hurried to her billet and packed a small backpack with essentials and then hurried around to the ambulance station where a steady stream of ambulances brought the wounded – and the dead - back from the front first aid station. She sought out a driver and after several tries found one who would give her a lift to the front. The driver explained that they were not officially allowed to take passengers, however a sweet smile from a beautiful woman won the day; on condition that she stay in the back and if there was any problem she was to say that she had sneaked in there when he was not looking; she agreed. She got into the back where there were two tiered stretchers and sat on one. As they got under way she lay back on the stretcher to ease her aching muscles and before she knew it she had fallen asleep to be wakened half an hour later by the driver announcing that they had arrived. She thanked him and wandered around to the First Aid station. She introduced herself to the resident doctor who, thinking she had come to help him, welcomed her with open arms. Under the pretext of checking the patients and acquainting herself with their injuries she used her visit to check all the wounded in the station and failed to find her brother but in the annex attached to the main station she was pleased to find one man who, recognising her, waved frantically. She walked over but failed to recognise him. He addressed her as My Lady and explained that he had worked on the estate. He expressed his sorrow on her loss, explaining that he had been on a mission with Sergeant Chumley when he was killed. He went on to tell her about her brother's bravery and of how they had wiped out a machine gun crew. He laughed.

> "After all that I had to take a bullet in the leg on the way back, but it may give me some time in Old Blighty"

She listened to him and thanked him for the information; she acted the part of a grieving sister – but she knew that her brother was not dead and that he must be a prisoner of the Germans; she hoped that they were treating his injury. She spent the rest of the morning helping the resident doctor who was inordinately grateful for the help. She was reluctant to leave him to his impossible task of treating the hundreds of wounded who passed through the station with only two other doctors and ten aids. They also had regular soldiers who had volunteered for the job of removing the dead or those too injured to be saved who were laid outside under cover and allowed to die in peace. She felt tears threatening as she watched all of those, mostly young, men waiting to die. She hurried away and made her preparations.

All morning there had been sporadic firing from both sides but when the expected onslaught did not materialise the Germans used the reprieve to resupply and get some much needed rest. During this lull Katie, who had made a flag of truce with a pole and half a sheet, scrambled up out of the trench with several soldiers attempting to stop her and marched towards the enemy lines. She had removed her cap and her golden hair seemed to blaze as the sun struck it. What little firing there had been petered out and she could hear quite clearly Germans calling to each other 'Das Zünden von Waffen' (Don't fire your weapons) and similar calls from the English lines, 'Stop firing'; she strode on, skirting the shell craters and trying not to notice the dead and decomposing bodies and body parts that were strewn everywhere. Reaching the German lines she was treated to several wolf whistles and comments, that with her limited German she fortunately did not understand. A German Captain reached up for her hand and assisted her down into the trench. She noticed that the condition of their trenches were better than those of the English – they were dry and had duckboards and strip seats at intervals. She did not get a closer look as the Captain, speaking in fractured English ushered her to the rear where several officers gathered around.

"Und vat do you vant, Mademoiselle?" He asked with a fractured mixture of several languages that strangely she could understand.

Catherine spoke slowly and clearly, and knowing that the Germans, as with the English, respected titles remarked, mostly in a mixture of English and French.

"Verzeihung, Captain, je suis Lady Catherine Chumley und ich glaube." She struggled for a while. "I am so sorry I cannot think of the words that I want." She felt herself blushing.

A German officer stepped forward.

"Pardon me Frauline, I am Oberst Kurt Langhans, may I be of assistance?" He spoke good English, albeit with a strong German accent.

Catherine let out a sigh of relief. "Thank you Oberst Langhans, I would be delighted. I am under the impression that my brother, Sir Christopher Chumley has been wounded and is currently in your field hospital – no doubt being given excellent treatment by your doctors," she added with a smile. "I would like to see him."

The Colonel looked at her for a long moment.

"Frauline, your brother is a very brave man and we Germans appreciate courage. However he did kill five of our men and ruined one of our machineguns - that we can replace but the men we cannot. Why should I help you?"

"Sir, I walked across a battlefield depending on German courtesy not to shoot me - in that I was correct. Now I am depending on that same gentlemanly courtesy from you to allow me to see my brother and if possible to take him home." She looked a picture of despair and desperation.

The Colonel studied the beautiful women in front of him for a while noting her doctor's uniform.

Frauline, I see by your uniform that you are a doctor, in that at least the English are ahead of us. I will let you find your brother, if he is still alive, and you may treat him. We will discuss what happens next later."

Katie asked to be taken to the first aid tent where she was introduced to the surgeon who was in the process of cutting off a man's leg. He nodded but did not offer to shake hands which were dripping with blood. She noticed him looking at her, testing for a reaction. She offered to assist him; an offer which he refused. He thought that the Englishman was at the end of the ward; she started her search walking along the lines of beds checking faces, but she could not find her brother. She noticed an orderly following her and stopped. He tried to tell her something but finally gave up and holding her hand led her outside to where a long covered annex was, he pointed to the end of the line of men. Walking down the long line of men she realised that they were here to die. As with the English doctors the rush of wounded was so great and the doctors so few that those who had little chance of recovery were set aside to die so that those who had a chance could live. She forced back her tears as she hurried down the line.

When she found her brother she was somewhat surprised to find him looking quite well. There was no blood dripping, no broken limbs; he seemed to be in better condition than most, although he was covered in mud, as were most of the others. She hurried to his side where he lay on the floor and whispered his name; there was no reaction. She examined him carefully and could see a groove running across his forehead and into his hairline. She followed the wound very carefully and felt a part of the scalp move and she realised that his skull was fractured and that his brain could be damaged. His pulse was thin and irregular. She hurried back to the surgeon who luckily spoke English and asked him if she could have her brother moved to a table so that she could operate on him. He nodded to the table next to his where a dead soldier had just been removed. He was interested to find out what this English female doctor could do. He instructed two orderlies to bring the Englishman. They laid the patient on the floor whilst they scrubbed the table free of blood with a strong smelling disinfectant; then they placed the sergeant on the table and left. Katie realised that she was not going to get any assistance, not because he was English but because they were too busy. Being close to the German doctor she asked him if she could use his instruments to which he pleasantly agreed. She removed her brother's top clothing- noticing how thin he had become; then she washed him with a weak dilution of the same disinfectant. She took a pair of rubber gloves from the supply near the German doctor and got to work.

>She removed the long hair with a pair of scissors and finding no razor she borrowed a scalpel and gently massaging a soapy layer over the affected area she very carefully shaved his head then applied more disinfectant; she could now clearly see the problem. The bullet had cut a groove across the scull, cracking an area the size of a teacup rim, It was not large but the depression had cracked across the centre causing the bone to depress onto the brain. Although she could see no damage to the dura mater she could see signs of cerebral fluid and blood around the edges of the bone. She reached across and borrowed a small hand drill and about a quarter inch drill, already sterilised, and proceeded to drill a small hole through the bone;

carefully retaining the bone fragments. She used a hooked probe which she gently threaded through the hole where she twisted it under the bone edge; using that she gently raised the bone until it was in the right place and taped it. Removing the probe she turned to see the German doctor watching her. She borrowed a small suction tube with an inch of rubber piping on the end and pushing it into the hole proceeded to draw off the small amount of blood and cerebral fluid that had collected there. Then she taped over the hole and placing a large soft pad over the wound she proceeded to bandage it in place. The whole process had taken just over five hours and she was exhausted. She washed and sterilised all the instruments she had used. She turned to thank the German doctor but he put his arms around her and gave her a hug.

"Gut gemacht, Fraulein' I am so glad that you had the time to do that; I am afraid I did not. She understood the words to mean, good work, and she was inordinately pleased.

She thanked the doctor for his assistance and had Christopher allocated a bed. Ensuring that her brother was as comfortable as possible she arranged a pillow on either side of his head so that he could not roll over and dislodge the dressing, then went in search of Oberst Kurt Langhans who she found in a tent with several other officers pouring over a map.

"Pardon my intrusion, Oberst Langhans but may I have a word with you?" He took her arm and led her outside, the rest followed. She assumed that they did not want her to see the map details.

"Did you find your brother, Frauline?" He inquired with a smirk.

"Yes, thank you Oberst. And I have operated on him and he is stabilised; now, with your permission, I would like to take him back to our lines," she requested with a smile.

Oberst Langhans took a step back as his eyes roved over her body. Catherine felt herself beginning to blush under his scrutiny.

"Lady Chumley, you haff invaded our lines…" He looked around for the expected laughter; which he got. "You use our facilities to treat your brother; a brother, who I might add kilt several of my men; now you have the audacity to request stretcher bearers to carry your brother back to your lines, where I haff no doubt he vill recover und attack us again."

"I can assure you, Oberst, that he will never be fit for active service again," she murmured with downcast eyes.

"That may well be the case, Frauline, however, all these things I haff done for you. As you English say, vat iss in it for me?" His eyes roved over her body as the rest of the group began to laugh in anticipation. Catherine was well aware of his meaning,

"So sir, German courtesy only goes so far," she stammered with a toss of her head.

Oberst Langhans smiled. "Frauline, we are a long way from our homes and our vives; we must take our pleasures vere ve may."

"So the gentlemanly German officer is quite prepared to cheat on his wife," she countered bitterly.

It was then that she noticed the scar that marked his cheek and a plan began to evolve. She had read that duelling scars were seen as a badge of honour since as early as 1825. They were known as Mensur scars also, amongst those who thought it stupid, as bragging scars. They were seen as a mark of their class and of their honour amongst university students who wore fencing masks that had gaps in strategic places where a sword could cut.

"I see, Sir, that you are a fencer of some note," she said, pointing to the scar that crossed his cheek.

He raised his hand to the scar and rubbed it, evincing some pride as he did so.

"Ja, Fraulein! I had the honour to be in the university team." He said proudly.

She smiled slightly, giving him an entirely wrong impression.

"Well then, Oberst, if you are in agreement I will fight you for it. My honour if I lose and you will help me get my brother to the English lines, if I win."

Everyone within hearing roared with laughter, slapping their sides and each other. Oberst Langhans could not believe his luck, however on reflection he assumed that the challenge was a method that this beautiful lady was using to ease her conscience, an excuse.

He danced around like a boxer. "You refer to pugilism, Frauline?" as he punched the air, playing to his audience.

"No, Herr Oberst, I refer to swords," she said with a smile.

"Ahhh! Let me get this straight, you are challenging me to a duel and if I win you vill spend the night in my bed? And if I lose I vill assist you in getting your brother to the English lines? Am I right?"

"That is correct Herr Oberst."

Again, Oberst Langhans could not believe his luck. Whilst everyone was laughing he called for his batman and sent him for his sword from his tent. Then turning to his friend. "Herr Brodman, would you please allow this lady to use your sword?"

"Jawohl, Herr Oberst,"

Within a few minutes they were facing each other with swords in their hands as a crowd gathered around.

Catherine felt the balance of the weapon and found it good, however, the weight was somewhat heavier than what she was used to. The guard was similar to those belonging to her father with a slight curve to the blade and a fluting, to allow blood to escape, along its length. It had no cup guard but a small cross piece included in the hand guard. She tried a few tentative swipes.

Herr Oberst was parading like a fighting cock, swishing his blade and showing off; much to the delight of his audience. Seeing his opponent standing at ease he strode towards her and casually attempted to knock the weapon from her hand with his sword. Caught somewhat unprepared, thinking that there would be some sort of protective clothing, perhaps a simple face guard; but no. Reacting instinctively she ran her blade alongside of his until the point locked on the guard and twisting against his thumb flicked the sword out of his hand sending it skidding across the ground. Katie walked over and picking it up handed it hilt first to its owner.

"It seems that I caught you unprepared Herr Oberst, shall we start again?" she said sweetly.

His face coloured up and the look in his eye told her clearly that if she made him lose face in front of his fellow officers her chances of getting her way was remote.

En Garde! He roared, taking up the classical stance, one leg forward, knee bent and left arm raised to the rear. She realised that the joking was over and that he intended to humiliate her. He rushed in intending to crush this woman who had embarrassed him. She tried a Coulé sliding her blade along his with the intent of establishing leverage as she had done at the start, but he was not to be caught twice. She made to counter, but with a shout of triumph he moved into a Moulinet, but she was ready; a moulinet, while flashy and impressive is slow since the action pivots around the wrist and elbow; she easily countered.

By this time quite a large crowd had gathered, most of them shouting encouragement to the young woman. She had repelled all of his clumsy moves and she knew that the bout was hers for the taking, but she gave ground knowing that if she embarrassed him in front of his officers she would never be allowed to leave let alone take her brother with her. The action ranged over a large area and she could see the sweat coursing down the Oberst's neck. Some in the crowd were placing bets. She was in a quandary. After twenty minutes she let her blade run up against his until their hilts met with a clang; their faces close to each other.

"Herr Oberst, it would appear that we are evenly matched, perhaps we should call it a draw. I am very impressed," she said, "I am afraid that I have misled you," she smiled, "I was chosen for the Olympics fencing team and I thought that I could beat you; but you are my match." She stepped back lowering her weapon.

Kurt Langhans had felt her superiority and was inordinately pleased that he had survived with his record intact – and he boasted to himself, having fought an Olympic champion – a slight exaggeration - to a draw. he knew that he would add that to his list of stories in the officer's mess for years to come.

He bowed to Catherine. "Vell done, young lady, you almost had me a few times, congratulations."

Then feeling magnanimous; "I'll send a couple of my men to fetch your brother," he bowed again and left.

The officer who had loaned her his sword, Herr Brodman, recovered his sword and in a low voice commented quietly in broken English.

> "Very astute off you Madam; unfortunately ve vill haff to listen to his version of this event for the next ten years." He bowed and retired.

A short time later two stretcher bearers arrived with Christopher.

One jabbered away in German pointing towards the English lines. His companion repeated his words in passable English.

> "Pardon. Frauline, my frient vants to know how ve get back once you reach der English lines?"

She appreciated their concern; both sides may well refrain from shooting a pretty woman but they may not be so concerned about two German soldiers.

"I promise you both that once I have my brother settled I will return with you." She reached out and patted his arm; he smiled his thanks.

She found her flag of truce where it had been discarded and brushed off the dirt; then thanking the men who had gathered around she mounted the parapet of the trench and helped the stretcher bearers to lift the stretcher onto the bank, They scrambled over and picking up the stretcher with Chris on it followed Katie into no-man's-land.

As before she could hear the shouted commands to hold their fire; but they already had. She led them around craters and less salubrious obstacles until they were within twenty feet of the English lines when a man with a rough Hampshire accent called for three cheers which rose with their delight.

"Welcome back, Miss, and you have the sergeant;" they exclaimed surprised.

Katie led them to the field first aid station and saw that her brother was safely into bed and then, to the German's relief she led them back to the German lines with the white flag billowing around her. She left them a few feet from their lines and walked back.

She hoped that all the movement had not disturbed the dressing, it seemed alright but she changed it anyway. The two English doctors gathered around to see what she had done and were impressed. She replaced the dressing and requested an ambulance to take her brother to the hospital where she normally worked and was lucky to find a place in an ambulance with four other men packed in – they were pleased to have her with them. The ambulance took off slowly avoiding the potholes and debris that littered the road.

CHAPTER EIGHT

The brightly painted Albatross fighters of Jagdgeschwader 1, Richthofen's Flying Circus were lined up on the German airfield twenty miles behind the front trenches. Richthofen, known to the British as the Red Baron lolled in his camp chair. The Iron Cross hanging from its ribbon gleamed in the morning sun. He was languidly smoking a cigarette as he observed his flyers.

Born on May 2, 1892 to a Prussian noble family, junker landholders, Manfred von Richthofen, learned to hunt at an early age.

Growing up in Silesia (now part of Poland) young Manfred learned from his father, a Uhlan career officer, and his maternal Schickfuss relatives. In the protected game forests, he and his brothers, Lothar and Bolko, hunted wild boar, elk, birds, and deer, collected and displayed their trophies in their castle. Later, the great ace would bring the same love of the hunt and love of victory to his aerial battles. He entered the Prussian cadet corps (military school) at age eleven, where he was an indifferent student. In 1911, he entered Uhlan Regiment Number 1, which he enjoyed; at least insofar as the opportunities it gave him to ride horses. He first fought on the Russian front, where the highlight of his cavalry exploits seemed to be capturing and locking up a Russian priest in his own bell tower. Transferred to the West, his Uhlan regiment spent several enjoyable, peaceful months in the rear areas. An assignment to the quartermaster corps didn't satisfy Richthofen. "My dear Excellency," he wrote, "I have not gone to war to collect cheese and eggs…" He asked to serve with a flying

unit. In May, 1915, his request was granted. Over the next few months his tally of British and French aircraft shot down over the battlefield mounted. After his sixteenth victory he was awarded the Pour le Mérite (the Blue Max). He then organized his own Jagdstaffel 11, dubbed by journalists The Flying Circus. He was without doubt a national hero and he revelled in that appellation. This day he considered that he had earned a day off, so handing over his Circus to his second in command he sent them off on a training flight. Leading the flight was one Manfred von Steiner who had previously been attached to the embryonic bomber command and he had a passion for blowing things up; being transferred to a fighter squadron did nothing to satisfy his urge to destroy. He had acquired a reputation for carrying a couple of light bombs in an attachment in his cockpit. He delighted in flying over enemy trucks and holding the small bomb by its fins and manoeuvring his aeroplane about thirty feet above the vehicle would drop the bomb and bank sharply to starboard to evade the blast. This practice was not appreciated by the Red Baron who considered it too stupid to get within range of rifle fire. He was not concerned about the pilot; his concern was for the aircraft which was, at that time, state of the art. During the briefing the previous day they had been told of a suspicion that the British were using the ambulances to ferry ammunition to the front, relying on the large red cross painted on the roof to protect them. Seeing the ambulance trundling along the road he never considered that it was going the wrong way to be delivering weapons; he positioned his aircraft about thirty feet above the ambulance and dropped his bomb banking sharply to port. He saw the bomb explode just behind the driver, killing him instantly. He saw the ambulance swerve into a ditch and overturn spilling wounded soldiers across the road.
Woops! he said to himself with a smile. Well, there are a few who won't be shooting at our soldiers. He had no regrets.

An army ambulance travelling along the same road about a mile behind came across the scene a few minutes later. The driver cursed the German flyers vehemently and long as he sorted among the dead and wounded. He saw the beautiful young woman dressed in a doctor's uniform and discovered a large bruise on the side of her head, she was unconscious. He lifted her carefully and carried her to his ambulance where he ordered a walking wounded to get off his stretcher and placed Katie on it. He walked back to the scene of the bombing and found another wounded soldier who was still alive, there were no other survivors. He tucked the wounded soldier in beside the young woman, there being no more room – they seemed to smile.

Reaching the hospital the orderly sent to bring in the wounded recognised Dr Chumley and she was soon being attended to by the duty doctor and given a bed. she regained consciousness half an hour later and despite all efforts to restrain her she insisted on walking out to the ambulance station to enquire whether there were any other survivors; she was informed that there had been one other survivor and that he had been taken to another hospital a few miles away because her hospital could not cope with the sudden influx of wounded after yet another bloody battle. She wanted to leave at once to try to find her brother. She knew instinctively that he was still alive, but her colleagues insisted that she rest for the day and perhaps she could look for her brother the next day. As there was no possibility of finding transport that day she tried to rest, but after an hour of twisting and turning she went back to work.

The following day, noting his colleague's distress the chief surgeon offered to drive her to the hospital where she hoped her brother was. When they arrived some hours later the resident doctor could not help her as he could not remember the patient's name; Katie rebuked herself for not writing his name on some part of him, however a short time later a nurses aid recognised her description of him and that of his wound and informed her that he had seen her brother and that his injury was considered so severe that he had been sent to Dieppe where a hospital ship was waiting to evacuate the wounded to England. She was pleased that he would get the best treatment possible but regretted that she had not seen him to satisfy herself that he was alright.

CHAPTER NINE

Of the sea Journey Christopher knew little; he was well looked after and when the ship docked at Dover he was taken to a major hospital where a week later he could sit up and accept food and drink. The doctors and nurses kept asking him for his name but try as he may he could not remember; they wrote on his record, 'John Smith, real name unknown. Amnesia caused by severe head trauma'. A few weeks later he was taken by ambulance together with two other mentally disturbed men to a convalescent home in Cornwall where he was fitted with a blue serge suit to denote his war-blown brains and given a small room complete with a bed, wardrobe and a toilet. Being not considered dangerous he was allowed to come and go as he pleased. People in the village soon became used to seeing these war damaged soldiers wandering around the village. He had been there three months when he happened to walk so far from the Home that he could not find his way back. Soon it began to rain and he was confused as to what he should do. He was taking shelter under a tree whilst he tried to come to a decision when a car pulled into the side of the road and a young lady got out and approached him. She smiled at him and studied his soggy appearance.

"Well, old chap. You are a long way from home aren't you?" He looked at her with feelings rising to the surface that had long been suppressed. He noted her pretty face with her mass of fair hair and felt that somehow he knew her, He was sure that he had met her somewhere, he smiled at her.

"I say, young lady, do you know me?" he asked.

Again she smiled. "Surely if I know you then you must know me." He looked at her a confused look suffusing his face.

"I'm afraid, young lady that is not necessarily true." His eyes sparkled with mirth. She noticed how blue they were; she also noted the scar that disappeared into his hairline.

"Will you tell me your name?" she asked.

He shrugged his shoulders. "I would if I could, Miss, but I am afraid that this," he pointed to the scar, "has robbed me of my memory, so I can't really tell you who I am."

"So what do they call you up at the Home?" she asked.

"Well, anything from John Smith to the Professor." He stammered slightly.

"Well, for the record my name is Susan. Susan Templeton." She held out her hand which he shook.

"Here, let me get you back to the Home," she said taking his arm. She helped him into her car where he apologised for wetting the seat. The car was a Ford, model T, which he had heard of but had not seen. It was a rather box-like machine with a fold back top which at the moment was firmly pulled up to keep out the rain.

"Oh! don't worry about that it was given to me when my mother died, it was an original when she was given it by my father, it is due for the scrap heap anyway." She listened to his voice and noted his refined speech; she liked the way he looked at her shyly yet respectfully; she had also noted that he said others called him the professor, which indicated that he was respected and educated.

They drove for a while, then she pointed to a small but very pretty cottage up on a small hill.

"That's where I live." She said; then on impulse.

"Would you like to come in and get dry and have a cup of tea? I can run you back to the Home afterwards, it is only a mile from here and I can easily get you back before they close the gates."

He looked at her smiling mouth and bright eyes and felt that same feeling of having known her.

"I would be delighted, if you have the time. It will be a pleasant change from the nursing home – but I really do not wish to put you out," he added with a smile.

"No trouble at all." She found herself drawn to this strange waif.

"It must be awful, not to remember anything, there must be family out there somewhere looking for you."
She saw the pain that her comment had caused him and resting her hand on his arm "I am so sorry, I am sure all will be revealed shortly." Now I'm sounding like a cheap thriller, she thought.

She pulled up at the cottage door and opening it she ushered him in. He studied her as she moved about setting out cups and making a pot of tea.

"Have you lived here long?" he asked.

"All my life really, since my mother died and I inherited this cottage; very lucky really," she added. She arranged the teacups and a plate of biscuits on a tray and went to lift it but her strange visitor jumped up and took the tray from her and set it on the table before them.

For an hour they chatted like old friends each one finding a delight in the other's company.

"Well, I must say this has been very pleasant, but now I must get you back to the Home or you will be in trouble," she laughed. "Perhaps we can do this again, if you want to," she hastened to add.

"Yes! I would like that very much," he smiled, reaching out to touch her hand.

Two days later Susan Templeton was sitting in her office, idly twisting a pen in her hand as she gazed out of the window, for the first time that she could remember she was unsettled, her mind confused; she could not get the image of the stranger who had entered her life out of her mind. She recalled his gentle smile and the way he looked at her with wonder, as if he remembered her from some time in his past – perhaps a wife? She thought not, but somebody that he missed from his past. She was restless and could not concentrate on her work as a legal attorney for a firm of lawyers, Masters and Masters; two brothers, Jason, the senior partner and Stephen his junior, who had started the company as soon as they had left university with their degrees. They were good bosses and treated her with respect. They were hard working and respected in the community, with the work piling up they were hoping to expand their company. She continued to gaze out of the window and was quite startled to see a Blue Man walk past in the street. She was not too sure whether she agreed with the appellation that the men from the convalescent home had acquired because of their light blue serge uniforms. She pushed the papers on her desk aside and turning to the senior partner asked if she could have the day off.

He looked up with a smile. "I have noticed that you have been very distracted since you arrived this morning; are you feeling alright?" he enquired with a concerned look on his face.

"No, Stephen, nothing's the matter with me, I just have a lot on my mind," she smiled.

"Humm. That sounds like love, we aren't going to lose you are we?" he said with the smile that he used when he teased her.

She laughed as she gathered her things.

She had no plan in mind and felt rather silly as she drove up to the front of the nursing home; several blue men were walking around the at Susan's obvious embarrassment. "You can't keep him hidden for ever – even if he is bald and short and has warts all over his face," he laughed.

"If that is an invitation, Jason, I accept on his behalf, "she laughed, "but watch your wives."
"Hmm, that good is he? I can't wait to meet him."

The following day she picked John up at the Home, he had refused to move into her cottage until they were married; also he had insisted that he had to have a name. They had bandied names around all evening and had at last settled on John Hanson; John had been her father's name and as she had been calling him that since they met it seemed an easy choice. Hanson had been her mother's surname before she married.

She explained about the Christmas party at her office and asked him outright how much money he had. John was not outraged as she thought he may well have been and answered.

"We do have a small pension which has accumulated over the months - I must confess to being embarrassed with you paying for everything. I really must look for a job. But I am not too sure what I can do; however, I am sure that I had a good education," then reverting to the original question.

"I believe my total assets to be in the region of fifteen pounds, and a few shillings. Not much, I'm afraid."

Susan laughed. "That will have to do. We need to get you some proper clothes; you can't turn up at the office in your Royal Blues," they laughed and hugged.

With their limited finances he could not afford a bespoke suit but he found a fine suit of dark grey that needed little alteration to fit his lean body. A new shirt and tie followed and he found a pair of black shoes that had the price reduced, with a pair of black socks thrown in. A haircut completed the picture of sartorial elegance.

When Susan picked him up at the Home, her heart seemed to lurch. All the staff, and many of the inmates turned up to see him off. He looked exactly as she pictured him, a tall broad shouldered gentleman – she could picture him in some stately home and she quailed as he took her hand.

They entered the office to find the party well under way as she circulated, introducing him to the bosses and the staff. Jason leaned toward her and with a smile remarked. "I see what you meant by your comment to watch your wives" Susan smiled with pride.

The party had been under way for over a couple of hours and the throng was pleasantly relaxed with the food and wine circulating when Susan happened to look to where the two partners were in a deep discussion and she noted that they were glancing towards where her fiancé was talking to the wife of Jason, she briefly wondered if he was worried for his marriage but she soon disabused herself of that thought; her fiancé was not the type to chase after other women, especially if they were married. As if he was aware of her thoughts he looked in her direction and smiled. As the party was breaking up Jason strolled over to where John was talking to the messenger and smiling at the messenger he asked if he could have a private word with John – the messenger drifted away.

John looked at Jason expectantly.

"So sorry to intrude, John, but may I have a word with you?" Not waiting for an answer he continued. "John, Susan has told us something of your problem – nothing private I assure you. But I understand that through war service you have lost your memory, I am sorry to talk shop at a party but we were wondering if you may have had any legal training?"

John smiled." I am sorry, Jason, but I really could not say, although I think that I have had a university education."

Jason noticed the easy way he used his Christian name, as well established men did. He wondered what his origins were.

"You remember nothing?"

"I'm afraid not."

"Well, being presumptuous and knowing that you are looking for a position we were wondering if you had any knowledge of legalities, so I wonder if you would consider coming to the office sometime next week and let us ask you a few questions, just to establish your credentials, certainly not a test," he protested.

John smiled. "Anything to jog the old memory can't be all that bad. I would be delighted, just name the day."

"Leave it to me, John, I will arrange it with Susan and she will let you know."

Susan dropped him off at the Home, very reluctantly, and drove home. The Matron saw him arrive and turned to the nurse.

"He won't be with us much longer I am sorry to say, he is such a nice chap." She sighed.

It was towards the end of the week when John received the message via Susan to meet with the partners. He was shown into Jason's office, where Stephen was already seated and he handed John a glass of cognac.

For the next hour they bombarded him with questions relating to their business, and strangely, to John, the answers came to mind quickly and accurately. They were particularly interested in his knowledge of the Laws of Tort, which as Jason exclaimed were the bane of his life. His mastery of the subject ensured that he was offered, not just a job but a partnership; on probation for a year. As Jason explained, he was taking a risk and he wanted to safeguard the company. John quite understood. They signed him over a five hundred pound retainer and established a starting salary of seventy pounds per month.

That evening he took Susan out to dinner in the most expensive restaurant in town – which happened to be the Queens Hotel in St Ives – splashing a large part of his retainer.

> "Now that I have a job we can be married." He cried sweeping her off her feet.

Susan glanced up at him from under her long eyelashes, "Are you sure that you would not rather marry that pretty receptionist at the Home?" She whispered.

He looked at her, his mind striving to place something, she regretted the ploy.

> "Stop that, you vixen," he laughed echoing a father that he could not remember.

The banns were called and they were quietly married in a small church in the diocese. There were only a few people attending, mostly from the office and a few friends from the Home. They settled into the cottage.

CHAPTER TEN

Fordingbridge Hall was a sad image of its former self. Several of the servants had been lost in the war and had not been replaced. The echoes of the war were still ringing through the halls. Charles looked towards his wife who he still loved with an undying passion; she had aged considerably since news of the death of their son had reached them; she seemed to have shrunk and her hair was now snow white; he thought it too early for a fifty-two year old woman, even with the burden that they both carried. She sat in her favourite chair looking out of the window down the long drive as if expecting her beloved son to appear at any minute; his heart went out to her. He was constantly endeavouring to get her interested in something to take her mind off her loss but even her passion for the greenhouse had gone and her once magnificent flowers were dying for lack of water. He reached for her hand and helping her from the chair led her to the conservatory to show her his latest invention. Noting the sad state of her flowers he had bought a long length of rubber hose and arranged a device to attach it to the water tap. He had laid it across the flower tubs and had drilled holes at each tub. He had to admit that it was not very elegant but it worked. He demonstrated it by turning on the water and saw how the flower pots flooded one by one.

"There!" He exclaimed. "Now you won't have to walk around with a bucket." She smiled gratefully and returned back to her chair without comment.

Catherine had constantly refused to believe that her brother was dead, in spite of all evidence to the contrary – she insisted that if he were dead she would know; she had talked her father into buying one of the new Ford cars, it was a model T Coupe manufactured in the new Ford assembly plant in Manchester. It had cost her father over 212 pounds, which he could ill afford, the war having supped up much of his fortunes. She also pleaded with him to pressure his contacts into supplying a comprehensive list of all those places where wounded troops were treated, including hospitals and most of those places that had been utilised for that purpose. His contact wished him well but warned him that the list was not necessarily complete, as many places had been utilised, church halls, council ballrooms and so on. He further warned that record keeping during the war was not the best. Armed with her list she loaded her car with several large cans of petrol and learning how to crank her car into life headed for the first hospital on her list where she checked every male, looking for her brother.

Catherine had been steady in her assertion that her brother was not dead and no persuasion would convince her otherwise Not even when a colonel of the Hampshire regiment had called at the Hall personally to inform his parents that Christopher Cholmondeley had been awarded the Victoria Cross posthumously for outstanding bravery in the face of the enemy where he had charged a German machinegun emplacement and destroyed it. There had been sufficient witnesses to the event to warrant the award. He informed the family that his award would be listed in the London Gazette and that the award would be presented to a member of the family at a parade of the Hampshire Regiment in one week's time, and he hoped that all the family would be there.

Richard assured him that they would. Katie had run from the room crying. "He's not dead – he's not dead. I would feel it." Her father had spoken to the Colonel explaining to him that his daughter refused to believe that her brother was dead and of the bond that they once had.

The colonel assured them that he fully understood as he had lost two boys in the war and that his wife had died of a broken heart. They shook hands briefly and retired to Richard's study where they sympathised with each other over a glass of brandy.

CHAPTER ELEVEN

A year passed and John Hanson could not have been happier. He still had no recollection of his past and was coming to the realisation that he never would. When their first baby arrived their cup did indeed runneth over. Jane was a beautiful baby, as she would be with such attractive parents. With her fair hair like her mother and sparkling blue eyes like her father, she was loved by all who came into her orbit. She was strong and healthy and displayed signs of outstanding intelligence, according to her doting parents.

John was now a full partner in the business and was delighted when approaching the office to notice that the company name had been changed from Masters and Masters to, Masters Masters & Hanson. He hurried in to thank the brothers and to receive their congratulations. With the arrival of Jane her mother had left the company, although she sometimes carried out work from home for them. When John told her of the changes that evening she brought out the bottle of wine that she had saved for his new birthday and they toasted his success.

Arriving at his office the following Thursday he found a note on his desk, it was from Jason; he walked into his office to discover Stephen already there. Jason looked at him and then at his brother.

John! Every year all of we Legal Eagles have a seminar in London; it is mainly to compare notes and to brush up on any advances in various legislations. Normally either Stephen or myself would go, however, on this occasion we think it would be a good idea if you went to represent us – you know; get to know the London mob and make contacts; you never know when we may need their help. What do you say?"

John was delighted and told them so.

"When does this shindig happen?"

"Well, John, it's Saturday. Rather short notice I know. If it is not convenient please say so - one of us can fill in."

"Look, I am sure it is alright but can I check with Susan?"

"Of course you can, why you don't pop home now and discuss it; then you can let us know when you get back."

Susan was very pleased for him, as he knew she would be and Friday saw him on the 8.15 train to London, where he signed into a hotel for the night then caught a taxicab to the place where the seminar was to take place. It had just started when he arrived and picked up his identity card to pin to his jacket. He found a seat at the front where nobody else seemed inclined to sit and listened to a series of boring talks until the midday break. He went into the dining room with several people who he had just met and ate an excellent meal notable for its paucity.

He circulated the crowd passing around his card bearing his name and that of the company that he represented. The hour break over they all traipsed back into the hall to hear a further four presentations. By this time John had met a few interesting people who he thought may be of some use as a contact in the future. They all had decided to congregate at a local pub, apparently the haunt of lawyers and solicitors. John, being at the front seats found some difficulty getting past those chatting in and around the doorway and he could see some of his new friends waving for him to hurry when someone tapped him on the arm.

"Hello, Christopher, how the devil are you? I haven't seen you for ages."

John looked the man over. "Do I know you?" he enquired politely, conscious all the time of the need to hurry.

"Don't you remember me? Johnny Parsons. I met you at the Hall," he added.

John thought that he was referring to the hall that they were currently in. "I am so sorry but I don't recall seeing you," he muttered as he hurried to catch up with the others. Johnny Parsons looked after him with a puzzled look on his face before shrugging his shoulders and walking away.

Catharine had driven as far as Edinburgh searching for her brother in every place on the list – and some that were not she added. Rolling up the driveway to the Hall she could see her mother still watching the drive for her son to arrive; she wiped away a tear as she unloaded the car of her personal things; leaving the rest and her car where it was. She was tired and saddened by all the dead ends that she had followed. She needed a break to refresh herself before setting out again on her quest, which she had no intention of abandoning.

The following day they and many of the servants, drove in a fleet of hired cars, a miscellaneous collection indeed; Most were Fords, all black, apparently because that was the only paint that would dry fast enough for Henry Ford's production line. They arrived at the parade ground of the regiment near Winchester and were led to the seats for honoured guests. All of the soldiers were in their dress uniforms and all the officers resplendent with swords and medal ribbons.

After a speech by the Colonel of the regiment Sir Charles stood up to receive the Purple ribbon and the medal and to give the eulogy. Jane and Catherine cried the whole way through the ceremony – Catherine partly through frustration because nobody would believe her that Christopher was not dead. After the march past the immediate family were invited into the mess where food and drink were served, but few had any appetite and did not stay long. Catherine was used to men staring at her, however one seemed particularly persistent. As they were walking to the cars he approached her and she prepared to give him a piece of her mind.

"I do beg your pardon, Catherine. I don't suppose you remember me do you?"

"No I do not." She snapped.

He persisted. "I was introduced to you and your family when I stayed at the Hall, before the war." He twisted his hat around in his hands and she suddenly felt sorry for him.

"I am afraid that I do not remember," she said gently, seeking to turn away.

"Oh! My name is Johnny Parsons and I was up at Oxford with Chris. Can you spare me just a minute? I think that I have news that may please you." he stuttered slightly. Feeling sorry for him she turned back to enquire what it was that might interest her. He led her to one side. "A strange thing happened to me a couple of weeks ago," he began. "I was at a legal seminar at the Dorchester, in London – and it was all very boring," he said with a smile.

"Pray, what has this to do with me?" she said with some asperity.

"One moment, please, Madam, as I was saying, I was at this seminar when a chap barged into me trying to get out. I turned to find Christopher, I am positive it was him, trying to pass me. I spoke to him but he said that he did not know me and hurried away," he paused.

"Go on. Go on! she shook him by the lapels of his jacket. "Are you sure that it was him," she cried out so loud that her father came hurrying back to her side a questioning look on his face.

"Father," she shouted joyously, this man has seen, Chris. I knew it all along but none of you would believe me." She was sobbing and the tears were flowing down her face.

Her father grabbed hold of the man, holding his fist under his nose. "Who are you and what the devil do you want? Coming here with some cock and bull story and upsetting my daughter." A crowd was gathering and Parsons became scared. He was about to turn away when Catherine threw her arms about him and led him to one side, her father followed.

"Look here, Miss, all I wanted was to tell you about your brother, I don't need any trouble, I have enough of that," he sniffed.

Catherine turned to her father. "Please, Daddy, let him speak, he is trying to do us a favour," she snapped. Her father was very wary of that tone and stood aside whilst Parsons repeated his story.
Catherine was ecstatic, her father, who thought it was some cruel ruse to extort some money from his daughter was all for calling the police.

Catherine had Parsons repeat his news again and again.

"Did he give you his address, or where he was staying – anything?" she pleaded.

"No, I am so sorry Miss but you could go to the Dorchester and check out who was there. It may help," he muttered.

Catherine threw her arms around his neck and gave him a kiss on the cheek.

"Thank you, Thank you," was all she could say, then. "Would you please give me your card so that I may contact you sometime?"

Parsons reached into his pocket and produced a card bearing the name of a company of solicitors and handed it to her. She thanked him again and let her father lead her away.

Her father cautioned her about getting too excited – "People change, my darling, and the mind has a great tendency to play tricks on us. However, I do hope that what he told us was true," he said wistfully. They decided to keep the news from her mother in case nothing came of it.

Catherine found waiting for the morning a trial, she could not eat, nor could she sleep. She arose early and dressed carefully before driving to the railway station in Southampton and catching a train to London where she managed to flag down one of the new taxicabs to take her to the Dorchester. As they drew up at the door, the doorman, resplendent in his uniform signalled a porter forward to collect her luggage. Discovering that she had none he enquired in a sarcastic voice what she wanted. Catherine, as had her mother had before her, announced in an imperious voice.

"My good man, my father, Sir Charles Chumley needs some information, please take me to the manager." She pushed past him and strode towards the reception with the totally abashed doorman trying to get ahead of her. He reached the receptionist before Katie and in a loud voice declaimed.

"Lady Chumley to see Mr D'Arcy, Matilda, please." He stood aside as the manager hove into view rubbing his hands obsequiously.

"Yes, My Lady, how may I be of service to you?"

"I believe you hold seminars here," she said. I have been informed that you held such a reception for the legal fraternity not too long ago.

"Yes, that is correct, Madam, I will get the Bookings Manager," he dashed away to return a few minutes later with an older man wearing pince nez, making his face look rather bookish.

"May I be of assistance, Madam?" he asked.

"Yes indeed you may. I would like to see the attendance list of companies and members of the legal seminar that you set up a while ago."

He opened a large leather bound volume that he had brought with him and set it on the counter. He turned the pages back until he found what he was looking for.

"This, Madam, is the list of companies attending and over the page are the lists of representatives."

She glanced down the page with the list of companies but could see nothing that struck a chord. Turning the page she scanned several pages of names of those attending, recognising none. She applied her finger to the list, causing the manager to frown his disapproval, and slowly drew it down the page. Nothing! She turned another page and did the same; concentrating. She noticed a very small tingle in her finger as it crossed, Hanson John. She began to get excited as the bold handwriting seemed familiar. She did it several times to make sure and taking a sheet of hotel paper she wrote down the name of the company, Masters Masters & Hanson and the address. Then thanking all and sundry she left and returned to the taxicab that was still waiting and returned to the station. She had a while to wait but discovered her success had given her an appetite which she indulged in the station café. She arrived back in Southampton three hours later and getting into her car set out for St Ives in Cornwall. It was late when she arrived so she booked into a hotel for the night and arose early to have her breakfast and drove slowly through the small town. It was not difficult to find the company that she was looking for; its new paintwork shone in the morning sun. She parked outside of the front door and entered. The receptionist had her desk alongside the new lift, which was obviously their pride and joy. She marched across the floor to the reception desk and in her best authorative voice asked to speak to Mr John Hanson. The receptionist looked slightly intimidated as she informed her that Mr Hanson was not in today and that he was having the day off – which seemed somewhat logical to Catherine. She asked for his home address. The young girl bit her lip and hesitated.

"I am sorry, Madam, but we are not allowed to give that information out," she said. "Can I pass on a message?'

"No, you cannot, Catherine stated flatly. I am his sister and I need to see him," she said authoratively, hoping that it was true.

"Well, in that case I suppose I can tell you," she said. "Perhaps I should check with Mr Masters first," she said, a look of uncertainty on her face.

"Oh! For goodness sake, girl, just give me the address," she snapped. The receptionist reached for a pen and scribbled the address handing it to her.

"I hope I won't get into trouble over this," she said.

"I'll see that you don't," muttered Catherine as she stormed out of the door. She had to ask directions as the address was a short distance out of town, but finally she saw a pebbled pathway leading up to the cottage. An old battered Ford, much like hers but much older stood beside the fence. Getting out of her car she stretched and walked up the path to the house noting the well kept garden and the mass of flowers. She knocked on the door and stood back, her heart was thumping in her chest. There was a long pause then the door opened and a beautiful young woman stood there with an equally beautiful child in her arms. She felt a surge of certainty as she noted that the baby looked exactly like her at that age. The woman looked at her enquiringly and Catherine knew she could easily love this woman.

"May I help you, miss?" she enquired.

"May I speak to your husband, please?" She stammered, the enormity of the moment making her quake.

"May I ask what this is about?" she asked a question in her voice; just then a man's voice echoed down the hallway.

"Who is it darling?"

Catherine recognised the voice and try as she may to hold it, tears of sheer joy coursed down her cheeks. Just then the man gently pushed his wife aside and stared at her, his face working and a radiant glow lighting up his eyes. They stared at each other for a long time then, in a voice full of joy and wonder.

"Poppet?"

And then they were in each others arms crying and laughing as his wife looked on, relief and joy spreading over her face.

THE END

www.ingramcontent.com/pod-product-compliance
Lightning Source LLC
LaVergne TN
LVHW040157080526
838202LV00042B/3195